FINAL JUSTICE

JOHN LEGG

WOLFPACK PUBLISHING
— EST 2013 —

Final Justice
Paperback Edition
Copyright © 2023 John Legg

Wolfpack Publishing
9850 S. Maryland Parkway, Suite A-5 #323
Las Vegas, Nevada 89183

wolfpackpublishing.com

Paperback ISBN 978-1-63977-819-5
eBook ISBN 978-1-63977-820-1
LCCN 2023931510

FINAL JUSTICE

1

"Travis Van Horn would never do something like that, Sam," Jace Coppersmith, marshal of Blanca, Colorado, said in surprise.

"Well, Jace, look at the telegram we just got," Sam Cosworth, Coppersmith's deputy, responded. "Says right there it's a fella named Travis Van Horn who's done the robbery. At least one other, too, I'd wager. It even says he has odd-red-colored hair, like you told me one time."

"It's something Travis wouldn't do, I'm tellin' you." Coppersmith was perplexed. He knew for certain that Van Horn, his mentor, would not rob a bank, yet a bank had been robbed and a man identified as Travis Van Horn was accused of having done it. He certainly wouldn't say anything aloud, but he thought that if—IF—Van Horn had done something so unlike him, he must have had a damn good reason.

"Got to disagree."

Coppersmith shrugged. "I might have to look into this."

"Come on, Jace, it's hundreds of miles out of your jurisdiction. Hell, it's in another state."

"Doesn't matter."

"Miss Lily won't like it."

"That might matter."

"Thought it would."

Coppersmith let it stew in his mind for a few days, wondering what he should do or even if there was anything he could do. Then another report came of a Travis Van Horn robbing a bank in Larned, Kansas, northwest of Wichita. That made up his mind for him. He had been a deputy marshal of Wichita, and Van Horn had many ties to the area.

"I'll need to be goin' to Kansas for a bit," Coppersmith said that night as he sat to dinner, as was usual, with Mayor Herbert Maddock; the mayor's wife, Eliza; and their daughter, Lily, who was the lawman's betrothed.

"Why?" Maddock asked, surprised.

"Some law business."

"What kind of law business?"

"None of your concern, Mayor."

"If it takes you out of Blanca, it is my concern," Maddock insisted. "You can't go off on some unknown business leaving Blanca unprotected."

"Sam'll be here, so the town won't be unprotected."

"It's far out of your jurisdiction, and as your boss, I must tell you that you cannot go off on some unknown quest."

"Then..."

"And what about me?" Lily asked.

"What about you?"

"You're just going to leave me?"

"I ain't leavin' you, Lily. I'm not gonna be long. I'll go

to Kansas, deal with my business there, and return as quick as I can." He was getting tired of this conversation already.

"How long will that be?"

"I don't know, Lily." He drew in a breath and let it out slowly, then said, "It shouldn't be very long at all." He was sure it was a lie, but hopefully only a little one. He had no idea how long it would take to track down Van Horn but he figured it would take some time, especially if his old mentor did not want to be found. And what would happen when or even if he was able to run the man down?

"But we're planning to get married soon."

"I know."

"Jace, have you really thought this through?" Eliza interrupted. She was always the most sensible of the Murdock family.

"Yes, I have, ma'am. For some days. It's something I have to do."

Before she could respond, the mayor said, "I'm afraid I'll have to tell you that you can't go, Jace."

Coppersmith picked up his napkin, gently patted his lips, and carefully put the cloth back down. Then he stood, pushing the chair back with his legs, pulled off the tin star he wore on his shirt, and tossed it on the table. He turned and headed for the door.

"Jace, wait!" Maddock said urgently.

Lily also called his name and rushed to him, catching him as he reached the door. "What about me, Jace?" she pleaded. "Us?"

"You'll have to decide that, Lily. I have important business to tend to, and I intend to do so. I'll be back as soon as I can. Hopefully it won't take long."

4 | JOHN LEGG

"It's another woman," Lilly snapped. "Isn't it? You got tired of me because of what I went through when..."

"There's no other woman, Lily." He took another deep breath. "This is none of your business or your father's, but I'll tell you anyway. A very good friend of mine is in trouble, and I aim to go help him."

"But..."

"That's all you need to know and all I'm gonna say, Lily. I reckon you wouldn't understand anyway. Good night."

"Jace," Eliza called. When he turned back, she added, "Good luck. Please be careful and return to us."

"I will try to do both, ma'am." He walked out and headed up the street to the small house he lived in, the one the city paid for. He almost smiled. He would have to get all his things out of the house before he left Blanca, not that there was much. Now that he was no longer the marshal, the house would not be his to live in.

He tracked down Deputy Sam Cosworth in the White House saloon. "Need to talk with you, Sam," he said.

The lawman put his beer down on the bar and gave Coppersmith a questioning look. "Sure."

"Not here. Finish your beer and meet me at the office."

"Be there directly, Jace."

———

"SO, WHAT'S UP, JACE?" Cosworth asked as he plunked down in a chair at the marshal's office. "Sounded important."

Coppersmith gave him a half-smile. "Reckon it is—for you."

"What in tarnation does that mean?"

"You'll likely be the new marshal of Blanca by morning, if not in an hour or two."

"What's goin' on, Jace?" Cosworth was confused.

"I quit. Just a bit ago, at dinner with the mayor and his family."

"You quit? What in hell for? You have everyone's respect in town, you're paid pretty well, and get a house. And best of all, you got yourself one hell of a pretty girl ready to marry you in a couple months. A man can't ask for much more."

"Sometimes there's things that're more important."

"What's more important than keepin' the peace in a fine town, and marryin' the mayor's pretty daughter to boot?"

"Helpin' a friend."

"That Van Horn fella?"

Coppersmith nodded.

"Come on, Jace, you really don't believe he ain't the one robbin' banks."

"Yeah, I do. Travis would not do such a thing." He paused. "If he is doin' these crimes, there's gotta be some reason."

"He wants the money. That's enough for most men."

"That's never been a big deal with Travis. Don't get me wrong, he likes money same as anyone else and makes sure he gets his reward money when he earns it. But he's never been greedy. Like I said, if he's doin' this, someone's makin' him do so."

"If he's as tough as you've said he is, how could someone make him rob banks?"

"Don't know, but it'd be something pretty bad. That's what I aim to figure out. Besides, maybe it ain't him, just someone usin' his name. Could be an outlaw he put away for a spell and is now out of prison. He might be

thinkin' to get back at Travis, by spreadin' lies about it
bein' Travis, maybe wearin' a disguise or wig and tellin'
folks durin' a robbery that that's his name. Hell, I don't
know, Sam. I'm just sure it ain't him."

"You goin' back to Wichita?"

"It's a place to start. If something bad happened to
cause him to do something like this, it seems likely, or at
least possible, that it might've started there, or
thereabouts."

"I still think you're a damn fool, Jace. I think that
friend of yours just went rogue. Maybe got tired of ridin'
hard trails, facin' tough outlaws and all kinds of other
dangers like gettin' shot at regular, and decided it was a
life he didn't want any more."

"Like I said, I don't believe that. But I will say this,
Sam. If it turns out to be true, I'll hunt him down and
make him pay, both for those crimes and for disappointin' me."

"Disappointin' you?"

Coppersmith nodded. "He not only taught me to be a
bounty hunter, but he taught me to be a man. An *honorable* man. And if he's gone bad, that'll go against my
grain and all that I believe in him—and myself."

"You're really serious about all this, ain't you?"

"You had doubts?"

"Reckon I did. Don't now, though. Anything I can do
for you before you leave?"

"Reckon not. If I think of anything, though, I'll come
find you."

"If I don't see you again, Jace, good huntin'." He rose
and shook Coppersmith's hand, then headed for the door
but turned back. "And I hope you're right that it's either
an imposter or someone's forcin' him to do this. I'd hate
to see a man you respect so much let you down."

"WHAT CAN I do for you, Mayor?" Coppersmith asked when he opened the door early the next morning.

"You need to vacate these premises."

"I know that. I'll be out by the end of the day, tomorrow at the latest, though I plan to be on my way by then."

"I mean now, Jace. You're no longer Blanca's marshal, and so have no right to stay in this house. I could've made you leave last night, but being a generous man, I let you spend the night. It's time to move on, though."

"And if I refuse to leave now?" Coppersmith's temperature was starting to rise.

"I'll have you thrown out."

"By who? Sam won't do it, even if you make him marshal. And I doubt you can find any man in town to try to do so. Now, go on home and leave me be. Like I said, I'll be out by tomorrow at the latest."

"I insist..."

"You can insist all you want, Herb, it ain't gonna change anything. Now, you're beginnin' to annoy me, and you really don't want to do that when I'm in quite a poor humor already. I know you're unhappy with me, and I'm purely sorry that you and Miss Lily are so upset with me. But I like to think myself an honorable man, and when a friend is in trouble, I've got to help. I'll be back as soon as I can. If you—or Miss Lily—don't want me back, let me know. I don't plan to stay in a place I'm not wanted, though Mrs. Maddock seems to have a different opinion on the matter than you or Lily. You want to contact me, telegraph me in Wichita."

"But, Jace, I don't want to..." The mayor stopped when he saw Coppersmith's face darken with anger. He nodded. "I'd like you to come back, even become marshal again if Sam doesn't mind. Can't say Lily will have the same feelings."

"Thanks, Herb." He closed the door before the mayor could say anything else. He dressed and headed out to a restaurant for breakfast. He spent an hour or so clearing out the house. It didn't take very long to have some men tote everything over to the Blanca Arms hotel. He figured that all of it would be lost, though he didn't consider it much of a loss.

He finally saddled his horse and was soon riding out of town, heading for Alamosa. That town wasn't that far, but Coppersmith had gotten something of a late start, so he pushed hard and arrived a little after dark.

He chafed when he learned it would be two days before a train would come along, so he paced around town, eager to be on his way. He considered just riding off, but Wichita was maybe five hundred miles and even at a good pace would take him two weeks or a little more to get there. So he waited impatiently. The train finally arrived, and he got himself a seat after making sure his bay gelding was as comfortable as he could be in a separate car. The trip was slow with a number of stops, but just a couple of days after he had left Blanca, he was riding his horse into Wichita having left the station only fifteen minutes before.

2

"WELL LOOK WHAT THE CAT DRAGGED IN,
Harry," Wichita Marshal Dan Quinn said with a laugh.
"Welcome back, Jace. Lookin' for your old job? I got an
extra badge right here."

"Not interested."

Quinn looked at him in surprise. "Something stuck in
your craw, Jace?" he asked seriously.

"Figured you might be able to tell me what's
goin' on."

"Nothin's goin' on," Deputy Harry Wallace said.
"What makes you think—"

"Shut it, Wally," Quinn said. "This about Travis?"

Coppersmith nodded. "I figure you know what's
goin' on."

"Yeah," Quinn said sadly.

"I don't think he's doin' this. Do you?"

"He is doin' it," Wallace said.

"I can't believe that."

"It's true, Jace."

"Must be something makin' him do it then. Travis

wouldn't just go out and start robbin' banks for no reason."

"That's a fact." Quinn swiped a hand across his face as if he had suddenly gotten tired and wanted to wipe it away. Before Coppersmith could say anything, Quinn said, "You look mighty travel weary, Jace. Go get yourself a room, tend to your horse, clean up a bit. We'll meet you in Fleming's and explain it all to you."

Coppersmith started to protest, then cut himself off. He nodded curtly, spun on his heel, and walked out.

Half an hour later, he was sitting at a table along with Quinn and Wallace in Fleming's restaurant. He didn't show much interest in eating, 'til Quinn prompted him.

"We can talk while we eat, Jace. I'm hungry and I expect you are, too, even if you're too damned stubborn to acknowledge it."

"You're an even bigger pain in the rump than I remembered, Dan."

"I try. Now order something and eat."

They ordered—pork chops, yams, corn, and biscuits for all. While they waited, Quinn said, "You're right. Travis would never just turn outlaw for the hell of it."

"What's the reason?" Coppersmith was in no mood to dally around the information.

"You remember Emil and Anneliese Bassmyer?"

"Sure. The Germans we helped and who took in Travis' little girl, Lizette."

"That's them." Quinn paused.

"So?" Coppersmith prompted.

"They're dead."

"Where's the child?" Coppersmith couldn't worry too much about a couple of people growing old and of no real importance to him.

"Gone."

"Gone? What the hell does that mean?"

"Just what you'd think. She's gone."

"Stop stallin', Dan. What happened?"

Before the marshal could say anything, the food arrived. All three men ignored it.

"Fella named Bucky Biddle and his band of cutthroats killed the Bassmyers and took off with Lizette."

"Where?"

"How the hell do we know?" Wallace snapped. "If we knew that, she wouldn't be there anymore. We would've brought her back a long time ago."

"You chased these fellas?"

"As much as we could."

"What's that mean?"

"Well, anything outside the city limits is out of our jurisdiction. That's up to county Sheriff Baxter Cartwright. He got up a posse as soon as the Bassmyers' bodies were found. But they'd been dead more than a day, so the trail was pretty cold. Cartwright combed the whole county, even by himself when the posse gave it up. Me and Harry searched as much as we could."

"And nothin'?"

"Nothin'. With more than a day's head start, rain erasin' tracks, and no direction to really look, we couldn't..." Quinn stopped, his anger rising along with his feeling of helplessness.

Wallace jumped in. "A few days later, we got a note. Biddle said he and his men had killed the Bassmyers and took Lizette. Said they wanted Travis to do some 'work' for 'em."

"Work like robbin' banks?"

"Yep."

"Travis was in town here?" That seemed odd to Coppersmith, if true.

"Nope," Quinn said. He finally cut off a piece of pork chop and forked it into his mouth. "We didn't know where the hell he was," the lawman said around the mouthful of food.

"So, how...?"

"We sent out wires to everyplace we could think of. Figured there might be someone out there who knew something. But we also figured that Travis would hear about it before too long since he was still bounty huntin' as far as we knew, and he was bound to come across a poster somewhere."

"He rode into town one day," Wallace continued for his boss, and we showed him the note. Wasn't much he could do but wait 'til he heard somethin'."

"Almost a week later," Quinn said, picking up the tale, "another note arrived. Somebody stuck it under the office door one night. By the time we found it, whoever it was, was long gone. Damn, I wish we had caught that son of a bitch."

"What was Travis supposed to do for 'em?"

"Note said to rob the First Savings Bank in Larned, leave the money in a canvas sack along a stream southwest of the town, and head back to Wichita. Said that if they saw anyone but him or he stuck around, they'd kill the girl. You've been out that way. There's nothin' there except flat, maybe a few buffalo wallows. Someone could see for miles, so there was no way to sneak up on anyone."

"Bastards," Coppersmith growled.

"That ain't a strong enough word for 'em," Quinn said.

Coppersmith dug into his food, using the cutting, chewing, and swallowing to take the slightest edge off his growing anger. "He didn't just hand off the money to some fella?"

"Nope, but he said he was sure there was someone nearby among the trees along the stream, the only place you'll find trees in these parts, as you know."

Coppersmith nodded.

"Note said to wait here 'til they had something else for him to do for 'em. So he waited. Couple weeks later, another note appeared one night. Said he was to rob the same named bank in Hays and leave the money east of there. A few weeks later, it was Ellsworth."

"As you can imagine, by this time Travis was steamin'," Wallace added. "He's a pretty even-tempered fella until he gets riled, and he was gettin' riled for sure. Makin' it all the worse is that he knew he couldn't do anything, couldn't even search for her. It was strange to him, too. He'd only met the girl once, a few years ago when you and he helped the Bassmyers. But he felt responsible for her."

"I don't know if he feels responsible for her really," Quinn said. "I think it's more that he wants revenge for the Bassmyers' killings. But, of course, he doesn't want any harm to come to the girl."

"Bad spot to be in."

"Yep. So why are you here, Jace?"

"Come to help him. I was sure he didn't do what he was accused of doin', but if he was, there had to be some reason, something out of the ordinary."

"Well, there was," Wallace said.

"Yep."

"So what're you gonna do, Jace?"

"I have no idea just yet. Where is Travis now, Dan?"

"On his way back from Ellsworth, I reckon. We got word a couple days ago that the bank there was robbed."

"Every bounty hunter in the west must be lookin' for him. We got word in Blanca. I was marshal there." When Quinn gave him a questioning look, he shrugged. "Long story. But there's paper out on him already."

"We know. We've been trying to keep it quiet as much as we can but, well, there's really little we can do."

The three fell back to eating while they thought. Finally, Coppersmith said, "Can you wire the marshal in whatever town is next in one of the notes? That way he could arrest Travis before he did the job, and the outlaws couldn't blame him. You could explain to the marshal there what was going on so he wouldn't really be arrestin' Travis."

"Thought of something like that," Quinn said. "Discarded the idea right off for a couple reasons. One, I can't know if there's a spy hangin' 'round there, wherever there is, or even maybe one here. Ain't even sure I can trust another marshal. Sad to say, not all lawmen are as honest and upstandin' as me and Harry. But the bigger reason is that it won't do any good, and maybe harm."

"How so?"

"If the outlaws think Travis really got arrested and might be going to prison, they'd have no more use for the girl. And if it was a staged arrest, Travis would be set free soon and we'd all be back to where we are now."

"Damn."

"Yep, that's the way I feel."

There was more silence other than the sounds of the men eating—and the noise of the restaurant—before once again Coppersmith said, "What if you got me as soon as you got the note. I could take off fast and wait at the next town he was going to hit."

"Same problem."

"Then how about if I go out and wait near where he's supposed to drop off the money?"

"Might work," Quinn said after some thought. "Could be mighty dangerous, though."

"I'm used to danger. So's Travis."

"Lizette isn't. You get caught out there, you'll likely end up dead, as will Travis when he arrives with the money, and they'll kill Lizette as soon as Biddle learns of it."

"We're between a rock and a hard place, ain't we, Dan?"

"Yep. Been tryin' to figure out something—anything—to do, but I ain't come up with anything."

"Maybe I can pick up the trail from where Travis dropped off the money this time," Coppersmith mused. "Maybe I can track the fella who picked up the money and he'll lead me to the others."

"That might work," Quinn said thoughtfully. "Be a lot less dangerous to all of you than the other. What puzzles me the most is where are they hidin' out? Like I said, there's nothing out there but a few trees along rivers and stream, so they don't have much of a place to hide."

"Could be livin' out there in a soddie. Nobody'd take notice of that," Coppersmith said.

"Likely anyone passin' by would. They'd stand out with no women around."

"Then maybe they're in some town. Maybe even movin' from town to town, stayin' a few days then movin' on."

"Might look strange with a bunch of gunmen wanderin' into town with a five-year-old girl," Wallace said.

"Maybe not. Depends on how many of 'em there are. For all we know, it's just Biddle and the fella who picks up the cash. If there's a bunch of 'em, most could camp outside town while Biddle and one or two others go into town with the girl. If anyone asks, they could just say her mother died, which would even be true in a convoluted way, and that they were takin' her to kin somewhere. Maybe they'd pick up some supplies."

"Have a drink or two," Quinn said sourly.

"Could be, but if he has any sense at all, he'd be mighty careful with rotgut. He or one of his men has too much and starts blabbin', things could go bad for him."

"So is that what you're gonna do, Jace?" Wallace asked.

"Ain't sure. Need to think on it a bit. Besides, I'd like to get a little help if I can."

Quinn looked hurt. "We ain't enough help?"

"You give up those badges and you'll be plenty of help. As long as you're wearin' those stars, there's not so much you can do."

"Good as done," Quinn said.

"Don't be a fool, Dan. You're a good lawman, so's Harry. You've kept the riffraff down to a minimum as best I can tell, and the people here like and respect you both. No need to give that up to go on what could be a fool's errand. Besides, you both have families."

"That's why I want to go. If my child was taken, I'd want anyone and everyone to help find her."

"It's what makes you a good lawman, and why you should stay here—to protect your young'uns and all the rest in town."

"You make me sound too damn honorable," Quinn groused. "You got anyone in mind for this help?"

"Reese."

"Travis' brother?" When Coppersmith nodded, Quinn asked, "Ain't he an outlaw? That's what I heard."

"No, he ain't. Another long story."

Quinn nodded. "How and where are you gonna find him?"

"Ain't sure. Wire Fort Smith and see if he's there. Or maybe ride down to Fort Smith, see what posters he picked up and try to follow him."

"Talk about a fool's errand."

"Could be, but I won't spend much time on it. If I don't find him in a few days, I'll go it alone."

3

COPPERSMITH WAS JUST COMING OUT OF A restaurant in Cottonwood Crossing, Kansas, when he almost ran into an attractive woman who was hand in hand with a young girl. "Pardon me, ma'am," he said, then stopped. "Miz Seaver?"

"Yes," the woman said tentatively.

"He's the man who helped us on the ferry that time," the girl said. "Threw that nasty man right off it." She giggled.

"That's right," Coppersmith said, kneeling in front of the girl. "How are you, Miz Annie?"

"I'm fine, sir."

"No need to call me sir, young miss. My name's Jace."

"Yes, sir." She giggled again. "Mr. Jace."

Coppersmith stood, grinning. "And how about you, Miz Seaver?"

"I'm well." She had relaxed, now that she had remembered who this hard-looking, well-armed young man was. "Still chasing outlaws?"

"Yes'm." He shrugged almost apologetically.

"Expect to find some in here in Cottonwood Crossing?" She smiled softly. "It's not known as a hotbed of outlawry."

"Just lookin' for six-year-old girls who like to rob banks." He looked at Annie.

She grew pale and looked close to tears. "I don't rob banks, Mr. Jace."

Coppersmith cursed himself for frightening the girl. "I know, Annie," he said hurriedly. "I was just joshin' you. You're a good girl, I bet."

"I am," Annie said adamantly, calming down.

Coppersmith winked at her, eliciting another giggle. He turned to Callie. "No, I'm just passin' through hopin' to find someone to help me help a friend who's bein' made to do some things that he doesn't want to do."

"Why is he doing that? Can't he just refuse?"

Coppersmith looked down at Callie's young daughter. He pulled a coin out of his pocket and handed it to the girl. "Why don't you go get yourself a piece of candy or two."

Annie looked at her mother, a question—and longing—in her eyes.

Callie hesitated a moment, then nodded.

The child happily ran off.

Coppersmith looked at Callie. "I didn't want the girl to hear. Might scare her. And I scared her enough joshin' with her a minute ago. My friend's doin' it because some outlaws are holdin' his five-year-old daughter hostage, threatenin' to kill her if he doesn't do their biddin'."

"That's awful."

"Indeed it is, ma'am."

"Do you mind if I ask what this fella's name is?"

Coppersmith could see no reason not to tell her. "I doubt you'd know him, but his name's Van Horn."

"Travis Van Horn?" Callie asked haltingly.

"Yes, that's right. Do you know him?"

Callie blanched. "I was married to him once."

Coppersmith was taken aback and speechless for a few moments, then asked, "Then you know Reese?"

"His brother? No. I know of him. He had taken off before Travis and I married. He had turned outlaw. Travis was still a farmer then, but he went down into the Indian Territory to find his brother. I tried to stop him, but he wouldn't listen. You men are such fools sometimes." She blushed. "He was gone for three years." A touch of bitterness edged into her voice. "I thought he was dead, so I remarried. Then he returned to my shock."

"I reckon he didn't stay around."

"No. He was about to kill my husband but decided to be a better man than that and so he left. He left the farm to me, then rode on. Some months later, though, he showed up again. He'd heard that my husband had taken to beating me. Travis taught him that it's not manly to beat women."

"Sounds like Travis."

"Haven't seen him since. Don't know anything about his brother. I expect he's still an outlaw."

"Nope. Travis did find him. Travis was a bounty hunter by then. He put Reese back on the right path. The man who taught Travis bounty huntin'—a fella named Nate Luckey—took Reese under his wing and taught him too. Travis trained me a few years ago."

"So Travis had...?" She faded to a stop.

Coppersmith realized the woman wanted to know but was afraid to ask. "Yes'm. He had helped some German families that were bein' put upon by some bad men from Texas. He met a woman named Gretchen Bassmyer and married her. Figured he'd try to settle down. A while later, Reese contacted him and asked for help in runnin' down the men who had killed Mr. Luckey. Gretchen gave birth while he was in the Indian Territories, and she died while birthin'. The Bassmyers didn't so much blame him as hated him for not bein' there when their daughter passed on."

A few tears had sprung into Callie's eyes. "So he took his daughter and left," Callie said more than asked.

"No. The Bassmyers took the child in, and Travis rode off, not wantin' to interfere. He didn't think he'd be a good father, especially to a newborn." Coppersmith smiled a little. "It was while he was on the move that he met me and trained me. I was a fractious little snot when he met me. But he trained me well, not only to be a man hunter but also to be a man. A good man I like to think."

"I believe that. So did he go back later and get the child?"

"No. He heard the Bassmyers and their friends needed his kind of help again, so of course he showed up. I played a small part in that. When it was over, the Bassmyers forgave him and told him to stay in Wichita and be Lizette's father. He met her just that once but knew he couldn't give that girl any kind of decent life. So off he rode again."

Callie offered a small smile. "Always leavin' the females behind."

Coppersmith was shocked but immediately realized it was not meant as criticism but said with sadness. He sighed. "Seems like. Never can rely on us men. Anyways, some outlaws killed the Bassmyers and took the child." A hard edge entered his voice. "They sent a note to the marshal in Wichita sayin' that they wanted Travis to do some 'jobs' for them."

"Illegal jobs."

"Yep. Said they'd kill Lizette if he didn't do what they wanted. He hadn't really been in Wichita in a while, but they figured Marshal Quinn could get hold of him. He did after a short while. So far Travis has robbed a couple, three banks for them."

Callie gasped. "And now you're after him to get the bounty," she said, her voice accusatory.

"No, ma'am. Like I said, I aim to help a friend, and Travis is the best friend I got. Best friend I ever had. I was marshalin' over in Colorado when word came that a fella named Travis Van Horn was robbin' banks in Kansas. I figured that it couldn't be Travis or, if it was, he was bein' forced to do so somehow. I came out to Wichita and got the story. Seems Travis brought a man named Biddle to justice a few years ago. Biddle just got out of prison. He'd heard about Lizette somehow and… well, you know the rest now. Travis just did a job for them so we figured it'd be a little while at least before they wanted him to do something again. I thought I'd take the time to try to find Reese to help out."

"And you thought you'd find him here?"

"Not really. But I knew he was from around here so I thought maybe someone would have seen him."

"He's never come around here in all the years since he first run off. Not that I know of anyway."

"I was afraid of that." Coppersmith sighed again. "Well, I reckon I'll go down the river to Fort Smith. I might catch him there. If not maybe someone there will know him and I can leave a message."

"I hope you find him, Mr. Coppersmith."

"Call me Jace, please."

"All right, Jace. But even more, I hope you can help Travis. My second husband turned out to be an unpleasant man, of course, as I explained, and I didn't miss him when he died. I care for my husband now." She blushed. "But I've always missed Travis."

"When I find him, I'll tell him."

"Don't you dare, Jace. No. Never," Callie hissed.

"All right. I—"

He was interrupted by a man, who asked in a harsh, though shaky voice, "Who's this, Callie?"

"My name's Jace Coppersmith," the bounty hunter snapped. "Who the hell're you?"

"Callie's husband. And though you're wearin' those guns and all, I ain't about to let you accost my wife."

"Does it look like I'm accostin' your wife? I'm standin' here talkin' to an old friend."

"An old—"

"Hi, Papa," Annie said, walking up, happily chewing on a piece of gum. "Mr. Coppersmith helped us on the ferry a long time ago. Made some bad men stop botherin' us."

"That right, Callie?"

"Yes, Mort."

"Sorry, Mr. Coppersmith was it?"

"Jace Coppersmith. Well, it was nice talkin' to you Miz Seaver. And you, Annie." Coppersmith touched the brim of his hat and strolled off. He didn't like Mort Seaver, but then he realized it was because he liked Callie Seaver. "Fool," he muttered. "Lily's waitin' for you back in Blanca, Jace Coppersmith. Maybe," he added ruefully.

———

THE NEXT MORNING, Coppersmith was heading to the stables when he spotted Callie Seaver again. "Mornin', Callie," he said with a smile.

"Morning, Jace," she responded, her face bright. "What're you doing up so early?"

"Gettin' ready to leave. Soon's I have some breakfast and saddle my horse."

Some of the brightness left the woman's face as she remembered his mission. "Good luck, Jace. I hope you catch those men."

"Thanks, Callie." He paused, then said, "I don't mean this to be forward, but if you ever need help, any kind of help, don't hesitate to call on me. Send a wire to Marshal Dan Quinn in Wichita or to me or Deputy... er, Marshal Sam Cosworth in Blanca, Colorado."

"I will do so, Jace," Callie said firmly.

"Say hello to Annie for me." With a tip of the hat, he strode off.

Callie watched for a few moments. "There's something special about that young man," she whispered. Then flushed.

4

COPPERSMITH WASN'T SURE WHERE TO START looking when he stepped off a small boat at the dock in Fort Smith, Arkansas. So he asked around until he found the federal marshal's office. A deputy looked up when Coppersmith entered the office.

"What can I do for you?" the lawman asked.

"Lookin' for someone."

The deputy laughed. "So is every other deputy marshal and bounty hunter who comes through here."

"Reckon I should've expected such a response," Coppersmith said, though he grinned. The grin faded. "I'm lookin' for a certain someone, a fellow bounty hunter. Last I heard he was workin' out of here."

"I know most of the man hunters 'round here. What's his name?"

"Reese..."

"Milstead?"

"Yep. That's him."

"What do you want him for?" The deputy's voice had turned harsh.

"He's an old friend and I got some news about a mutual... friend."

"Good news, I hope."

"Nope. Bad news."

"Mind tellin' me what this trouble is?"

"I do mind. It ain't any of your concern. Not to seem unfriendly, but what I got to tell him is for him alone."

The lawman stared at him for some moments, then nodded. "I can respect that."

"He in town?"

"I believe he is. Come in a couple days ago with a few prisoners. And a few bodies. Was still here the last I heard."

"Know where?"

"Likely at the Hangtown saloon near Rogers Ave. and Fifth Street." He pointed in a general direction.

"Obliged, Marshal."

It didn't take long for Coppersmith to find it, but Milstead wasn't there. He found a nearby livery stable and left his horse, then found a room and finally a restaurant. After eating a barely edible meal, he headed back to the Hangtown, where he waited a spell, sipping on a beer. A couple hours later, he gave it up and headed for his hotel room.

He spent the next two nights in the same way and was beginning to think Milstead had left town when the man he sought walked into the saloon. Milstead stopped when he saw Coppersmith, went to the bar, got a bottle of tanglefoot and two glasses and sat at the table across from Coppersmith.

"Jace Coppersmith, isn't it?"

"Yep."

Milstead poured two glasses of whiskey and pushed one across the table. He jolted down the contents of his glass in one gulp, then filled the glass again. "Come to town figurin' on tryin' your luck huntin' outlaws in the Nations?"

Coppersmith took a sip of whiskey and put the glass down. "I come lookin' for you."

Milstead's eyebrows raised in surprise and question. "What in hell for?"

"Travis is in trouble and needs our help."

"What kind of trouble?"

"You ain't heard?"

"No," Milstead said, shaking his head. "I've been out on the trail for a spell. Just got back a few days ago."

"He's been robbin' banks," Coppersmith said.

Milstead laughed. "That's a good one, Jace. Had me goin' for a minute there"

"It ain't a joke, Reese."

Milstead stopped with the whiskey glass halfway to his mouth and put it down. "If that's true, there's somethin' else goin' on. There ain't no way in heaven or hell Travis would take up such a thing."

"I thought the same, but I found out it's true. And, like you, I figured if he was doin' it, he was bein' compelled to do so."

"He is, right?"

"Yep. You remember I told you Travis was a father but left his little girl with the Bassmyers?"

"Of course."

"Well, an outlaw named Biddle killed the Bassmyers and took the girl. Lizette's her name. He and his gang are holdin' her, threatenin' to kill her if Travis doesn't do what they want."

"So they have him robbin' banks." It was more a statement that a question.

"Yep. The marshal in Wichita, Dan Quinn, is a friend

of Travis, but he hasn't been able to run the bastards down. Neither has the Sedgewick County sheriff, a fella named Cartwright. I know Quinn is a good man. I don't know about Cartwright. Quinn says Cartwright has been lookin' hard to find Biddle."

"How'd you get mixed up in this? As I recall, you were huntin' some other outlaws and I heard they were headin' to Colorado, with you on their trail."

They did, and I did. Found 'em and taught them the error of their ways in a way they'd never forget."

"Dead men don't do much harm."

"True enough. Anyway, in the doin' I wound up savin' the daughter of the mayor of a town called Blanca. When it was all said and done, I wound up as marshal of the town and betrothed to Lily."

"You been a busy fella. That don't explain how you got involved with this."

"Bein' the marshal, I got word that some fella named Travis Van Horn was robbin' banks. So far, Quinn and Walton have managed somehow to keep the paper on him to a minimum. But that can't last. Anyway, like I said, I thought the same as you did. So I turned in my badge"—he grinned a little sourly. "Second time I've done that—and headed to Wichita to see what was goin' on and how I could help."

"That where you learned about Biddle? He's a bad one, I hear."

"He is, I reckon, though he's a cowardly bastard if he resorts to usin' a five-year-old girl to force a man to do something. And yes, there's where I heard about him. Travis had just pulled a job and was headin' back to Wichita, so there'll be some time before he's ordered to do another. I thought about tryin' to search from where he left the last of the money but decided that might not work. There's been plenty of rain, so any tracks likely would've been washed away."

"So you came to get me."

"Yep. I reckon you'd want to throw in with me."

"You ain't wrong. I'd say let's leave now, but night's comin' fast. First thing in the mornin'?"

"I'll be ready."

———

THEY PULLED out just after dawn, heading up along the Arkansas River. With the erratic nature of boats on the river, they figured they could make better time on horseback, though it was a far piece. Still, unencumbered as they were—with just a packhorse with them—they would not be delayed. They would stop every few hours for ten or fifteen minutes to let the horses graze a little and drink, then they'd be off again. Nights were short with camps quickly made and then deserted in the mornings.

A little over a week later, they rode into Wichita. They took the rest of that day and the night to clean themselves up, eat well, and catch up on their sleep. Then they met with Marshal Dan Quinn and Deputy Harry Wallace.

"Where's Travis?" Coppersmith asked when he entered the office.

"Keepin' to himself as he has been since all this started."

"Where is he? I want to talk to him."

"Best to let him be, Jace."

"But—"

"He's right, Jace," Milstead said. "I reckon he knows we're here and will do whatever we can. No need to add to his burden. If he wants to talk to us, he'll get in touch."

"That's about the size of it," Quinn said. "Now, I hate to pry, but you're Travis' brother, right, Reese?"

"Yep."

"But when Jace introduced you, you had a different last name. I thought Travis and all his brothers and sisters had the same ma and pa." It came out as a question.

"You wouldn't be malignin' my parents would you?"

"Hell, no. We don't know each other, you and me, but Jace will tell you I'm as loyal a friend to Travis as Jace is."

Milstead nodded. "I figured that was the case." He sighed. "I was a foolish fella when I was young and didn't like Travis orderin' me about, which, as the head of the family after Ma and Pa passed on, he had every right to do. So I up and left one day while he was off on a trip to town." He shook his head, anger at himself growin'. "That wasn't such a bad thing, since I'd be out of his hair. What was bad was that I just left the two youngest ones by themselves when I took off. I've been mighty ashamed of myself for that ever since."

"Like you said, young and foolish. Many of us do damn fool things when we're young," Quinn said.

"That's something I can attest to," Coppersmith added fervently.

"Anyway, I got myself involved with a gang of outlaws. Travis, bein' the damn fool decent man that he is, come lookin' for me, even though he had heard that Brewster Hook was a real bad man. He was just a damn innocent farm boy then, but that didn't stop him though. He wound up gettin' the stuffing beat out of him by some other outlaws. They took him outside of town and left him there, naked as the day he came into this world, with a six-gun that had only one round in it."

"Damn," Wallace gasped.

Milstead gave him a crooked grin. "He was wonderin' what to do when a fella named Nate Luckey came along."

"He's the one who was killed and you asked Travis to come down and find the killers. When Gretch—" Quinn clamped his mouth shut.

"Yep," Milstead said quietly. "Nate took him in and taught him to be a man hunter. Travis and Nate took care of the boys who had left Travis for dead, then hunted down Hook and took care of him and his men. All except me, that is. He convinced me that I was an idiot. By that time, it wasn't hard for him to do. But instead of bringin' me back to Cottonwood Crossin' to face justice, he rode off by himself, a capable bounty hunter now. Nate took me in and taught me the way he had Travis. I ain't sure, but I think Travis told officials around Cottonwood Crossin' and Fort Smith that I'd been killed along with the rest of Hook's gang. We decided, though, that it might be a good idea if I was to change my last name just in case someone hadn't gotten word." He grinned. "Of course, anyone who knows Travis and sees me would know him and I are kin, what with this hair and all."

"You have one hell of a family, Reese," Quinn said with a shake of the head.

"That's fact. He told me he had left the two young'uns with relatives, but I never heard anything more about 'em."

"I believe they've grown into a responsible young man and a respectable woman. I also think they want nothin' to do with Travis. Or, especially you, Reese."

"I'm a little surprised about Travis, but not at all about me. After all, I was the one who abandoned them."

Milstead sighed. "Well, that's all in the past. As much as I might regret some of the things I've done, I can't change them. And I've tried to make up for my sinful ways as best I can."

"From what we hear, you've done an admirable job of it," Quinn said. He took a deep breath and let it out slowly. "Now that we're all here and ready to bring this to an end, we need a plan. Anyone have one?"

"It ain't much of one, but it's all we have for right now," Coppersmith said. "But I think I should do what I suggested and ride out to wherever Travis is supposed to leave the money next time and follow the tracks of whoever picks it up. Whoever it is has to be close by."

"That's mighty dangerous—for you and for Lizette," Wallace said. "Once you get away from the few trees along the river or stream, there ain't much cover."

"Reckon that's so. You have a better idea? Any of you?"

Silence gave him his answer.

5

At the knock on the door, Coppersmith and Milstead drew their revolvers and cocked them. They moved to stand against the wall on each side of the door. Milstead reached out and opened, the door, remaining behind it.

"Holster those pistols, boys," Van Horn said as he stepped into the room.

Milstead and Coppersmith rotated the cylinders of their six-shooters until the hammer rested on an empty chamber, then holstered them.

"Drink? Something to eat?" Milstead asked. He waved a hand at the table on which stood a couple of beer-filled mugs and some sandwiches.

Van Horn ignored him. "What the hell're you doin' here, Reese?"

"Havin' a beer and chowin' down on some roasted beef, compliments of the nice saloon next door."

"That ain't what I mean."

"I know Travis, and you damn well know why I'm here."

"And you," Van Horn asked, turning to Coppersmith, "what are you doin' here?"

"Same answer you got from your brother."

"I don't want your help, either of you," Van Horn snapped. "Just ride on back to wherever you come from and stay out of my business."

"No," Milstead and Coppersmith said in unison.

"You've got no business here."

"Like hell we don't," Coppersmith said evenly.

"You won't do anything but cause trouble, trouble I don't need right now."

"Sit down, Travis," Milstead said. "There's a chair for you and we have enough sandwiches for us all."

"I ain't got the time."

"Where else you gotta be, Travis?" Coppersmith asked. "Unless you got another message from those bastards."

"No," Van Horn grumbled. He hesitated, then sat. "I don't need you boys here messin' things up."

"Messin' what things up?" Milstead said more than asked. "All you're doin' is their biddin'. You got no place to run those bastards down."

"And you do?" Van Horn snapped.

"Not yet we don't," Coppersmith said. "We just got here."

"Well, there's nothin' you two can do. Nor Quinn and the others either."

"So you just plan on robbin' banks for these fellas forever?" Coppersmith asked.

"Only 'til I get Lizette back."

"Eat," Milstead ordered. "And how're you planning to do that? You have no plan either, I reckon. If you did, you would've put it into play already."

Van Horn took a bite of a sandwich. "I'm thinkin' on it."

"And now we're thinkin' on it, too," Coppersmith said. "I ain't the smartest of fellas, but between us three and Dan and Harry, we got a better chance of comin' up with something instead of you by yourself when your mind is occupied with how safe Lizette is."

"This is none of your business."

"Ah, hell, Travis, don't be such a damn fool," Coppersmith said. "Of course it's our business. Reese is your brother and I... well, I ain't sure what I am to you, but you're the closest thing I have to a best friend. That makes it my business as well. The Bassmyers were good people. I learned that when I helped out with those men who were tryin' to run roughshod over them a few years ago. And if only for them bein' killed in the way I heard they were is reason enough for me to hunt down the bastards who did it."

"But Lizette ain't your kin."

"She'd hardly yours, Travis," Coppersmith said. "You never paid her no mind." Seeing the angry look that crossed Van Horn's face, he added, "You did right, Travis, leavin' her there with the Bassmyers. You were right, too, in realizin' you weren't cut out to be a father to a little girl. None of us here are, though I was thinkin' of makin' a stab at settlin' down."

"Besides, Travis," Milstead said, "I *am* kin to that little girl. I'm your brother and as such I'm her uncle and while I've never seen her, she's my blood. That means a lot to me even if it don't matter any to you, as seems the case."

"Why you son of—" Van Horn started to say as he half rose out of his chair. Then he settled back down. He chewed on another bite of his roasted beef sandwich, trying to calm his temper. Finally, he said, "I ain't much given to apologizin' as you boys know, but you're right, both of you, and I'm obliged for any help you can give me to get the girl back. But I don't know what you can do. I've been rackin' my brains to figure something out, but nothing's come to mind."

"Well, your mind's been stuck on the danger Lizette's facin', so you can't think straight right now," Coppersmith said. "But now me and Reese are here, we'll come up with something. We'll get that little girl back, Travis."

"I hope to high heaven you're right, Jace, but I just don't see how that can be done."

"Well, I had the idea of headin' out to where you're supposed to drop the money off next time and waitin' to see whoever shows up. I'd follow him back to whatever hole Biddle is hidin' in."

"Dan told him that'd be foolish. Once he gets out from the trees along whatever stream is there, he's got nothin' to hide him, except maybe a buffalo wallow now and again."

"That's a fact, Jace. You should know that. You were raised out there."

"I know," Coppersmith grumbled. "But I—we—need to do something."

"Gettin' killed ain't something that needs doin'," Van Horn said, then added, voice showing some anger, "And doin' something doesn't include gettin' Lizette killed."

"Oh, I hadn't realized that, Travis. I just figured that if I ran down the outlaws and they killed Lizette, then I'd have done something important."

Van Horn's eyes bulged as rage ripped through him. Then he took a deep breath and let it out slowly. "Sorry, Jace."

"It's all right, my friend. But I'm open to any suggestion either of you might have."

"I also had the idea of headin' to whatever town you were supposed to rob next and talkin' to the local law, but that has its own problems, and probably worse ones."

"I reckon it does."

There was silence as the men thought as they ate. Then Milstead said, "Maybe talkin' to law dogs in those towns might not be a good idea, but what if me and Jace ride out, startin' with places you robbed banks, Travis, stoppin' in towns, lookin' for some rough fellas travelin' with a little girl."

Van Horn thought that over for a bit, then nodded. "Something like that might work. As long as you two don't do anything but get your rump back here to get me so we can go out and end things."

"That'd be no problem, brother."

"Then we're in agreement?"

Milstead nodded; Coppersmith said, Yes," then a moment later, said, "No."

Both Milstead and Van Horn looked at him.

"I mean no offense to either of you," Coppersmith said, "but as has been noted more than once in various places, that head of hair of yours, Reese, makes you look an awful lot like Travis, especially to someone who doesn't know either of you very well. Biddle gets word that some fella with orangish red hair is pokin' around, well that might not be good for Lizette's safety."

"I'll be careful. I…"

"No, Reese," Van Horn said. "Jace is right. Somebody sees you and thinks it's me, Lizette's in immediate danger. And if they know I have a brother, that'd be just as dangerous to her."

"Well, what the hell am I supposed to do? I didn't come all the way up here from Fort Smith to sit on my ass and do nothing." Anger, annoyance, and frustration fought for dominance on his face.

"Never fear, brother, we'll figure out something for you to do."

"Damn well better," Milstead groused as they all went back to eating.

Between mouthfuls, Van Horn asked, "You said you had considered settlin' down, Jace?"

"Yep. Believe it or not, I was a lawman again. Town marshal in a place called Blanca, over in Colorado. Had me a fiancée, a gal named Lily. Her pa is the mayor there."

"Goin' straight for the top, eh?" Milstead said with a chuckle.

"Why not?" Coppersmith offered up a small grin.

"So what happened?"

"Well, I heard that somebody named Travis Van Horn was robbin' banks all over Kansas. I didn't think it was true, so I decided I needed to look into it."

"Why?" Van Horn asked.

"Well, if it was you doin' it for yourself, I was gonna attempt to bring you to justice."

"You think you could take me?" Van Horn asked, a touch of hardness in his voice.

Coppersmith grinned some more. "Well, I just might. You are gettin' a mite long in the tooth for a bounty hunter. I thought I heard your bones creakin' when you sat."

Van Horn let out with a laugh. "That's the first time I've laughed in a couple months. But you could be right. It wouldn't be easy, though."

"To be honest, Travis," Coppersmith said seriously, "I

would not want to find out. If you had gone outlaw, I would've tried though."

Van Horn nodded. "I'd not like to face you in a fight, either, Jace. So you came out here?"

"Yep. Like I said, if you'd gone outlaw, I'd have tried to bring you to justice. I didn't think you'd do so, but I had to know. So I turned in my badge in Blanca—"

"Just like you did here."

"True, and as you did here, too. My resignin' in Blanca did not go over well, though. And I figured that if you were doin' it because you were bein' forced to, I was here to help."

"Well, thank you, Jace. Despite my complaint when I came in here tonight, I do appreciate it. And how'd you get into this, Reese?"

"Jace came down to Fort Smith to get me. Figured I'd want to help, too. I didn't want to but Jace talked me into it." A smile spread across Milstead's face.

"Hell, if it had been left up to Reese," Coppersmith said, "we would've left that night and rode straight on to here without stoppin'."

"I ain't surprised. He is a testy snot at times, but since I got him out of that gang some years ago, he's turned into an almost halfway decent fella. Gotta keep an eye on him, though. You never can tell when his orneriness will come out."

They all laughed.

"Anyway, I turned in my badge and headed this way."

"There's more to it than that."

"Yep. Before I left, my fiancée let me know that she did not approve of me runnin' off to help some friend who's maybe gone rogue." Coppersmith shrugged. "Maybe I'm a fool, but I figured friendship for a man who'd pulled me up from that wretched life I'd been livin' was more important to me than a woman who couldn't understand that."

"Think she'll change her mind when you get back?" Milstead asked. "*Are* you goin' back?"

"Don't know the answer to either. But I doubt I'll be goin' back. Blanca's a good place, and it would've made a nice place to get married and raise a family, but with things the way they were when I left, I doubt I'd be welcomed back with open arms, either by Lily or her pa."

"How'd you end up as marshal?" Van Horn asked.

"Lily was taken by some outlaws. I rescued her. The marshal in town and a couple of his deputies tried to kill me and took off. The mayor made me marshal as well as temporary county sheriff, and I took off after the culprits. Found 'em and took care of them, too. Then I went after Rutledge."

"He's the one killed those old folks here, wasn't he? The reason you turned in your badge?"

"Yep. I had been followin' him and tracked him to near Blanca. I stopped in town, learned that the mayor's daughter had been taken, and went to see if I could bring her back."

"No wonder the poor girl wanted to marry you," Milstead said. "You're her knight in shinin' armor."

"Bah. That was early last winter. The weddin' was planned for next month. Reckon that's off."

"Sounds like you regret comin' here," Van Horn said.

"Nope, Travis. I regret things ended the way they did in Blanca, and I'm sad. She's a good woman mostly, though a little capricious. But sometimes there are things that're more important."

"Like friends," Milstead said.

"Like friends."

6

THEY ATE IN SILENCE FOR SOME TIME BEFORE Coppersmith stopped with his sandwich halfway to his mouth. He put it down. "There's something we never thought of 'til now. Or at least you've not said anything, Travis."

"What's that?"

"How do we know Lizette's still alive?"

Van Horn froze, eyes widening. "Son of a bitch," he said. "You're right, Jace, I never thought of that."

"Your mind's been occupied."

"I hate to say it, Travis, but she may not be. Once Biddle found out he could control you with the threat of harmin' her, he had you hooked and you'd keep on doin' his biddin' in the hope of gettin' her back."

Van Horn's face darkened with rage. He tried to speak but could only sputter a few disjointed words.

"We need to find out," Milstead said. "If she is, we'll figure out a way to get her back. If she ain't..."

"We're free to hunt those scum down," Coppersmith finished for Milstead.

"How're we gonna do that?" Van Horn managed to squawk.

The three stared at each other for some minutes, then Milstead said, "Maybe if we..." He stopped, shaking his head.

More silence fell upon them before Coppersmith said, "The only thing I can think of is to leave a message asking for proof that Lizette is alive."

"How would we do that?" Van Horn asked after giving it some moments' thought.

"Write a note asking for proof and stick it in the bag of cash when you leave it next time. Tell Biddle that if he doesn't show she's still alive, you'll assume she's dead and come after him."

"If she is alive," Milstead said, "such a threat would likely seal her doom," Milstead said. "He might figure you've done enough for him and decide to end things. He'd kill her and move on." He looked around at the sour faces of his two companions. "Besides, how would he prove she was alive? Bring her to the drop-off point? That's the only way it can be done."

"Dammit all," Van Horn snarled.

"I reckon we ought to be goin' on the idea that she's alive, at least 'til we find out differently," Milstead said.

Van Horn and Coppersmith nodded glumly, and they fell into impotent silence again.

A few minutes later, Coppersmith turned his head slowly from side to side, as a notion began to form. Finally, he nodded. "I think I have an idea of how Reese can also go from town to town lookin' for some rough fellas travelin' with a little girl."

"You said that won't work because of our hair," Milstead said, unhappily.

"That's true, but that's part of the idea. 'Course you might not like it, Reese."

"If it'll help my brother get that little girl back, I'll do damn near anything."

Coppersmith smiled. "Figured you'd say that. Still..." He smiled crookedly.

"Well, what is it, dammit?"

"Cut your hair real short or, better, shave it all off and be bald for a while."

"I ain't gonna do that," Milstead snapped. "That's ridic—" He paused. "I don't much like the idea of bein' bald-headed, but it makes a heap of sense." He nodded. "Damn right I'll do it."

"Thanks, Reese," Van Horn said humbly.

"Thanks ain't needed in this case, brother." Milstead's face was tinged with embarrassment.

"And since there's paper out on you, Travis, you best keep out of sight as much as possible." Before Van Horn could object, Coppersmith said, "I know you've been doin' it, Travis. I figure most folks in Wichita won't go spillin' the beans about you bein' here if they see you, which they likely will now and again, but there's probably a few who will, or might. Since most folks know or think that Dan is a friend of yours, they might figure to tell some lawman elsewhere that you're here in hope of gettin' a reward. Besides, Biddle might have spies around town."

"Damn," Van Horn snapped. "You got any more annoyin' ideas?"

"Yep. I think we need to talk to Dan. Harry ain't his only deputy, but we don't know if we can trust 'em. If Dan says we can, that'll make things simpler."

"What do we need the marshal for?" Milstead asked

"With paper out on Travis, there'll be lawmen and bounty hunters lookin' for him."

"Yeah, so?" Van Horn said.

"So, we can't afford to have someone capture him. Just like we can't trust lawmen elsewhere to be in on our plans or help us by arresting him on fake charges, we can't worry about him bein' taken by others. You're good, Travis, maybe the best, but you can't always prevent bein' bushwhacked."

"Again, yeah, so?"

"So," Milstead said slowly, catching up to the idea, "we need a deputy, whether real or not, to 'arrest' you."

"What good will arrestin' me do?" Van Horn demanded.

"We're not gonna arrest you, dammit. Just pretend. Hell, not even pretend. We'll just be escortin' you back from where you leave the money, though we won't join you 'til we're well away from there. This way, if another lawman or bounty hunter shows up, we can say you're in our custody."

"There is some risk," Coppersmith said. "There's a chance if that happens, those men might somehow get word back to Biddle that you've been arrested. But I think it's worth the risk. I doubt if any of those men will do that. They'll more likely try to take you from us."

"Which is another problem," Milstead said. "They decide they want to try that, there'll be gunfire, and there's no tellin' what'll happen then."

"I'm confident enough we can withstand it, especially when Travis will also be armed, though we'll keep his pistols hidden 'til we learn those others' intentions. I don't think that'll happen, though. Sorry to say, Travis, but you ain't worth that much. At least not yet. Only a couple hundred bucks."

They thought that over for a spell, then Van Horn said, "Like we've already said, if Biddle thinks I've been arrested, it'll likely give him reason to kill Lizette." He bit back a flash of rage. "If he thinks I've been arrested, he has no reason to keep her alive."

"Maybe this ain't such a good idea," Milstead said.

"You have a better idea?" Coppersmith asked.

No one said anything until Van Horn asked, "So how does this work?"

"Say Dan trusts one of his deputies or deputizes one of us, we can ride out to where you're supposed to leave the money. Not anywhere close enough, of course, to spook whoever's collectin' the money. Then he rides back with you as his 'prisoner.' One of us could do it as a bounty hunter, but other bounty hunters or lawmen might be reluctant to shoot a tin star rather than another bounty hunter."

"You're not as mutton headed as I thought, Reese. You can even think sometimes." He offered a tight grin, which quickly faded. "It'd be best if it was a bounty hunter escortin' me back here."

"Why?" Coppersmith asked.

"A city marshal has no jurisdiction out there, especially if the robbery didn't take place in his town."

"That likely means one of us," Milstead said.

"Likely it does."

Coppersmith said, "Dan trusts the county sheriff. Maybe he could deputize someone, leavin' me and Reese to roam."

"That might work," Van Horn said after a minute of contemplation.

"I'll talk to Dan," Coppersmith said. "Where're you plannin' to stay, Travis?"

"Ain't sure. I've been movin' around a bit. That might

not be a good idea, though, now that I'm a wanted man." The last was said sourly.

"You still on good terms with the Germans after what's happened?" Coppersmith asked.

"Yeah, why?" he asked, then caught on and shook his head. "No, I ain't puttin' any of 'em in any more danger. They've had enough trouble. I ain't about to bring 'em more."

"But—"

"No, Jace. No."

Coppersmith nodded. "You got somewhere to stay then?"

"Just a few abandoned places I've been usin'. I'll see if Dan has any ideas of where I can hang my hat for a spell."

"Then we'll do it?" Coppersmith asked. There were nods all around.

"Obliged. To both of you. If—"

"There's the door, Travis," Milstead said. "Use it before we all get weepy."

Van Horn nodded once and left.

"You all right with my idea, Reese?" Coppersmith asked when Van Horn was gone.

"Like I said, I don't cotton to the idea of bein' bald, but if it'll help, I'm fine with it."

"Best get yourself a new hat first thing." Coppersmith grinned.

"What's that?"

"You shave off that mop of hair and you'll need a hat two sizes smaller."

Milstead chuckled, then nodded. "Reckon I will." He paused, then said, "Won't my gettin' rid of my hair cause some questions around town?"

"Why? What do you mean?"

"Well, it's been mentioned more than once since I got here how much me and Travis look alike because of our hair."

"Yeah, so?"

"Won't it raise some eyebrows if all of a sudden there's only one orangish-haired fella in Wichita?"

"Could be," Coppersmith said after a little thought. "But Travis hasn't been around much, at least where people can see him. Anybody notices, they'll just figure there was only one of you to begin with or if they knew there were two, they'll figure one of you has left."

Milstead nodded.

An hour later they had tracked Marshal Dan Quinn down at Reed's restaurant. Each pulled out a chair. "Mind if we join you?" Coppersmith asked, sitting.

"Suppose I said no?" Quinn said, not slowing down his eating.

"What'd you say? Didn't hear you," Milstead said.

"Figured. Order something. The city'll pay for it."

Quinn waited until his two companions had started eating before he asked, "I don't figure you boys're here because you enjoy my company over supper. What's up?"

"Reese is gonna shave his head so he can search some towns without givin' away that he's related to Travis."

"I won't know who you are so I can't arrest you," Quinn said with a smile. "Of course, since I won't recognize you, I might just figure you're a troublemakin' outsider and arrest you anyway."

"You throw me in jail you'll have to feed me every day."

"True. Sounds like a good idea. Anything else? You look like you have more to say."

"Ask more than say," Coppersmith said. He explained

their plan to have a "lawman" escort Van Horn to and from his forced robberies.

"Sounds like a good idea. I should've thought of it."

"You got other things on your mind, like keepin' law and order in the town."

Quinn nodded. "There must be something else."

"Me or Reese could do it but we figure that other bounty hunters might be more inclined to shoot other bounty hunters than lawmen."

Likely true, but you can never tell with bounty hunters. I know a few and they're all troublemakers." He grinned. "I can deputize either or both of you."

"Could run into problems if we're near some other town. A Wichita marshal or deputy has no jurisdiction outside the city."

"You have an idea?"

"Maybe. I believe you said yesterday that you trusted the county sheriff...what's his name?"

"Baxter Cartwright."

"Yeah. Can you trust him with Travis' safety?"

"I think so, but I can't be a hundred percent certain."

"Any of his deputies?"

"Most of 'em are honest lawmen, but you never can tell when there's reward money involved. Even a couple hundred bucks looks good to a man making fifty a month if there's little risk."

"So it wouldn't be a good idea to entrust Cartwright or one of his deputies to do it."

"I would not suggest it."

"Can Cartwright be trusted enough to deputize me or Reese without raisin' too much of a fuss?"

Quinn sipped coffee as he thought that over. "I think so but I'm not sure. I'll have to sound him out."

"I'd be obliged if you did. Worst thing is that me or

Reese, or maybe both of us, will do the escortin' as what we are—bounty hunters—and fight off anyone else who tries to take Travis from us even if he is wearin' a badge."

"Don't need that kind of trouble."

"Nope."

"Meet me here tomorrow for supper. Meantime, make sure you're ready and that Travis stays out of sight."

"He knows that."

Quinn smiled ruefully. "Yeah, I know. I worry about him, though. Me and Travis go back quite a few years. He's been a big help to me more than once. I'd sure as hell hate for anything to happen to him. I'd hate it even more if that child is hurt."

"Us, too," Milstead said.

Quinn rose and slapped his hat on. "Enjoy the rest of your meal, boys. See you tomorrow." He sauntered out.

"You trust him, Jace?" Milstead asked as he watched the lawman leave.

"Yep. He's backed our play a few times. Does what he can while stayin' within the bounds of the law."

Milstead nodded.

7

"I AIN'T TAKIN' THE DAMN THING," MILSTEAD said as Sheriff Baxter Cartwright tried to hand him a Sedgewick County deputy sheriff's badge. "You were a lawman before, Jace. You take it."

Coppersmith sighed and took the badge. As he pinned it on, he asked, "Are you okay with this, Sheriff?"

"Yep. I ain't happy protecting a bank robber, but I'm even less happy to have some scum nab a child and use her to get her father to do those robberies. I want Biddle and all the men with him caught. And soon. This has gone on long enough."

"We'll do our best."

Outside, Coppersmith said, "You could've taken this. Or another one."

"Hell, wearin' that thing'd give me the shakes." Milstead chuckled. "Besides, I'm doin' my part by cuttin' off my hair."

"Reckon I can't argue with that. When're you plannin' to get it done?

"Soon. Dan said he'd send a barber he trusts over to the hotel and have him do the cuttin' there."

"See you later, then."

They split, Coppersmith heading for Quinn's office, Milstead for the hotel.

———

JACE COPPERSMITH RODE into the small town of Pratt, near Pawnee Creek. He felt a little odd here, seeing as this dot of a town was not far from Walnut Creek, where Travis Van Horn had found him and rescued him from a life that did not seem to have many years ahead of it, and those would have been mighty rough. Pratt was smaller than Walnut Creek, or at least Walnut Creek when he left it. Unlike Walnut Creek, however, Pratt appeared to be growing. While some sod houses still stood on the outskirts of town, the homes in town, and a few the prospering businesses, were of brick or of wood hewn from trees along the banks of the creek and planed in the nearby sawmill.

He had taken a turn as an "escort" for Van Horn once, and it went off without trouble. But all the men involved figured it'd be a while before Biddle ordered another robbery, so Coppersmith had decided to roam some towns looking for Biddle, or at least information on him. A bald-headed Milstead was doing the same northeast of Wichita.

Coppersmith pulled up in front of the marshal's office, dismounted, and tied his horse to a hitching rail, then went inside.

"Can I help you?" a young, skinny though competent looking man asked.

"The marshal around?"

"I'm the marshal," the man said flatly.

"Like hell you are. Now where's the marshal?"

"Who are you to be askin'?"

"Deputy Sheriff Jace Coppersmith of Sedgwick County."

"You got no jurisdiction here in Finney County." The young man had smugness written over his face.

"Now, look, sonny—"

"Sonny?" the deputy exploded. I'm older than you are!"

"In years maybe. In wisdom, you got a long way to go, sonny." He emphasized the last word. "Now, tell me where the marshal is."

"And if I don't?" The smugness had returned. It dropped in a real hurry when he found himself starting down the muzzle of a .44-caliber Colt Army.

"Shoot you in the head, though considerin' what a pumpkin head you are, it might not do much damage. I'm willin' to find out, though. Are you?"

"Marshal Quimby is either on patrol or in one of the saloons."

"He favor one of them over the others?"

"Caber's."

"Where is it?"

"Three doors down on other side of the street."

Coppersmith slid the revolver away. "See, now that wasn't so hard, was it? You'd do well to treat others with respect, at least 'til they show they don't deserve it. Like you should've done here. Tryin' to make folks believe you're a hard case when you're not is a good way to get yourself killed." Angry, the sheriff left.

Coppersmith figured that checking the saloon first would be easier than hunting through the town looking for the city lawman, especially since he didn't know the man. He was lucky. Quimby—who Coppersmith identified by the glint of light on the badge when the lawman moved in a certain direction—was at the bar chatting with a few businessmen. Coppersmith stopped not far away and stood, watching and waiting.

After a short wait in which Quimby barely looked at him, Coppersmith had had enough. "Excuse me, gentlemen," he said, "since you seem to be occupyin' the sheriff's time and I need to speak to him, and he doesn't seem to notice me, I aim to start shootin' you fellas one by one 'til you either leave or Marshal Quimby realizes talkin' to me would be in his best—and your—interest."

Indignant, the businessmen turned, ready to berate whoever was so audacious to challenge them this way. Then they saw Coppersmith's armaments and the hard look on his face. All politely but very hurriedly bade farewell to the lawman and left.

"This better be good," Quimby said in a huff.

"Now I know where that deputy of yours got his annoyin' habit of disrespecting people he just met."

"We respect people who deserve it. And we expect to be respected ourselves. Sendin' those men packin' does not show me respect."

"You don't deserve respect. You're a goat turd who thinks he's something special because he's the marshal of a pissant town in the middle of nowhere."

"I'm the law here and—"

Coppersmith tapped the badge on his chest. "And I'm the law in Sedgwick County. I know I'm out of my jurisdiction, but bein' a fellow lawman ought to get me respect just for that alone. Now quit tryin' to get me to believe you're a tough fella and answer my questions. If you'd done that right away, you'd still be talkin' to your fat, pompous pals."

"Ask," Quimby said through gritted teeth.

"Have Bucky Biddle and his men caused any trouble in these parts lately?

"No."

"Have you seen 'em?"

"No."

"Thanks, you've been a great help," Coppersmith said sarcastically. He turned to leave, then turned back. "Oh, I don't respect you."

"I don't need respect from a young punk from another county. You're just an arrogant kid who doesn't deserve respect despite wearin' that badge."

"That so?" Coppersmith slapped Quimby across the face. "Maybe that'll change your attitude next time someone comes along." He looked around the saloon, which had grown completely silent. "If the City Council appointed this buffoon to the job, find somebody else. If you folks voted this shit pole into office, vote him out, immediately. He's a blight on your community." He walked out, angry at himself for losing control. It was something he did not want to make a habit of. He should have just walked away and let the no-account marshal have his little victory. Coppersmith would never see him again.

He had planned to spend the night in Pratt but that would not be wise now. Tiredly, he mounted his horse and rode out. He spent the night—another miserable one, he thought disgustedly—out on the prairie, and the next day pulled into Lake City. Though the marshal was not as unfriendly as the one in Pratt, he wasn't very helpful either, so Coppersmith moved on.

His next stop was Medicine Lodge. He tied his horse outside the marshal's office and, tensely, walked inside. "Marshal?" he asked.

"That's me, Marshal Seamus O'Rourke. You seem surprised."

"I thought the marshal would be out patrolling the town."

O'Rourke grinned. "That's what deputies are for. They patrol the town. I sit here on my duff drinkin' coffee. Speakin' of it, you want some?"

"Sure."

O'Rourke chucked his chin toward a small potbellied stove on which a large pot sat. A couple of tin mugs hung from pegs on the wall nearby. Coppersmith grabbed one, filled it, and tasted it. He grimaced as he took a seat.

"Great ain't it?" O'Rourke said with a laugh.

"Great if you want to tar your roof." He set the mug down.

"So what can I do for you, Mr. ..."

"Deputy Jace Coppersmith, from Sedgwick County. I'm trackin' Bucky Biddle."

"Rough character that one," O'Rourke said after a staring at Coppersmith for a moment, wondering if the name was real.

"I know."

"A little out of your jurisdiction, aren't you?"

"Yep," Coppersmith said. "But Biddle committed some rather nasty crimes in my county. So I'm lookin' for him even if it is out of bounds legal-wise."

"By yourself?"

"Yep."

"You're a fool, but that's your business. Why come to Medicine Lodge?"

"Hopin' to pick up his trail again. I was following it north of here for some time and lost it durin' those storms we had a couple weeks ago. I'm checkin' wherever I can think of. Since Medicine Lodge is near the Indian Nations, I thought he might've been through here."

"Thank the Lord, no he hasn't. I don't need that kind of trouble."

"Nobody does, Marshal. Not anyone with sense anyway."

"When it comes to men like Biddle, I got plenty of sense," O'Rourke said.

———

COPPERSMITH FINISHED SADDLING his horse the next morning after an evening spent filling up on good food and sleeping on a soft, comfortable mattress. When he was done, he paused, then shook his head. He pulled the tin star off the front of his shirt and dropped it into the depths of a saddlebag.

"Sorry, Sheriff," he muttered, "but the damn thing was annoyin' and it wasn't doin' any good. Now I'll try it my way."

Five minutes later he was riding east out of Medicine Lodge. Just before noon two long, hot, dusty days later, he rode into Harper. He was tired, hungry, and irritable. He stabled his horse and got a room in a boarding house, then set about getting himself cleaned up.

A bath, shave, and then a decent meal improved his spirits a little. Then he tracked down the town marshal chatting with a clerk in one of the two mercantile stores in town.

"A minute of your time, Marshal, whenever you're free." When the lawman nodded, Coppersmith added, "I'll wait outside." As he went and sat on a chair outside watching the people, he wondered how long it would be before the marshal came out to talk to him.

To his surprise, the lawman came out less than ten minutes later. The marshal learned against one of the posts holding up the roof of the portico. "What can I do for you, Mister?" he asked.

"Lookin' for my brother-in-law," Coppersmith lied. "Tall, skinny fella travelin' with a couple other fellas and a little girl. I was supposed to meet 'em here but I was delayed a few days in Medicine Lodge, and I figured they were through here several days ago. If I know when they were here, I can maybe move faster and catch up to 'em sooner."

The lawman studied Coppersmith for a minute, then asked, "Why would a few men be travelin' with a young girl? Sounds mighty suspicious."

"Her parents died a couple weeks ago. Ford's takin' her to live with her grandparents in Missouri," he said, seeing no reason to use Biddle's real first name.

Again, the lawman stared at Coppersmith, who stared right back. "They must be movin' fast. They went through here more than a week ago."

"Damn. Reckon Ford's tired of hauling a child around. He was never fond of young'uns. Trouble is, he was the only one available to bring her to her grandparents. Thanks for lettin' me know, Marshal."

"You headin' out right away, I reckon?"

"I'd like to, but dark ain't far off. Now I know that they've been through here and when, I can move faster myself. But traveling in the dark won't help me catch 'em. I'd have to move mighty carefully. I'll head out first thing in the mornin'." It irritated him that he had to wait, knowing where Biddle and Lizette were heading, but what he had said was true.

Once more the lawman glared at Coppersmith, then nodded once. "Good luck catchin' up to 'em." He turned and walked away.

Figuring he would be watched, Coppersmith went back to the boarding house and stayed there cleaning his weapons until it was time for supper. He ate well, then returned to his room and took to his bed early.

Coppersmith was up before dawn and was pleased to find that although she was unhappy about it, Mrs. Callahan, the owner's wife, had breakfast ready for him as she had promised the night before. He ate hurriedly, grabbed his saddlebags and Winchester, and headed out.

He saddled his horse and rode out, touching the brim of his hat to the dark figure of the marshal standing in the shadows of the land office across the street from the livery stable. Then he was moving fast.

8

A FEW MILES OUTSIDE HARPER, COPPERSMITH picked up what he thought was Biddle's trail. There had been some rain two days ago and prints were left in the mud that had dried. With little traffic on this road, the tracks were not disturbed. At least he hoped they were the tracks of Biddle and his men. Prints showed six horses, one of them with deeper impressions as if a large man was riding the animal or a man was riding with a five-year-old with him. At least it seemed that way to him. The thought angered Coppersmith anew. He hoped he was right—it meant the child was still alive.

He pushed on hard, hoping to close in on the outlaws. If he could find out where they might have a hideout in this area, he could go back to Wichita and bring back help to take down the outlaws.

He came upon two old campsites, which he thought the outlaws had used, though he could not be certain. But if the tracks he had been following were the right ones, his quarry had stayed here.

Late in the evening two days later, he arrived at

Milton. He followed the usual routine—stabling his horse, finding a room, having a meal. In the morning, he went to the marshal's office right off, hoping to catch the lawman there before he started his daily patrol of the town. He was in luck.

"What can I do for you?" the marshal asked.

"Have a couple fellas with a little girl been through here lately?"

"How would I know that?" the marshal asked suspiciously.

"If you're a good lawman, which I assume you are, you'd know about it."

The lawman almost grinned. "Why do you want to know?"

"My brother-in-law and a friend are takin' the girl to live with her grandparents in Nebraska. Girl's parents died recently. My brother-in-law, lovely gent that he is, doesn't want to raise the girl, so he offered to take her to Nebraska."

"Don't know as if I believe you, son."

"Don't give a damn whether you believe me or not, Marshal. I just want to know if they passed through here and if so, when and which way was they headed."

"I don't like your attitude, sonny."

"And I don't like yours." He glared at the marshal, who glared right back. Coppersmith sighed. "Then how about this? These fellas and a couple other goat-humpin' bastards, who I figure waited outside town, made off with the girl and I'm after 'em."

"Bounty hunter?"

"Sometimes. This is personal." When the lawman cocked an eyebrow at him, he said, "The girl ain't exactly kin, but she's a good friend's daughter. He can't chase after 'em just now, so I'm doin' so."

"Why didn't you say so in the first place?"

"Sometimes hard to tell if every lawman is honest. Some I've known have had connections with outlaws. Hell, some of 'em have even been outlaws."

"I resent that."

Coppersmith shrugged. "I got to think of that girl's safety."

The lawman nodded after a few seconds. "And you aim to fight these boys by yourself and take back the girl?"

"That's my intention."

"Might be tough."

"I've done tough jobs before."

The marshal stared at him for a few moments. "They were here three days ago. Didn't stay the night, just rode in, got some supplies, and left. The girl did look a little ragged from the glance I got of her. They headed northeast out of town."

"Toward Wichita?"

"Yep. I don't know why, but I think they're gonna turn off somewhere before they get there."

"Obliged, Marshal."

"If you're tellin' the truth, and I ain't entirely sure you are, good luck in chasin' down those scum."

Coppersmith nodded and left. He had a hurried breakfast, saddled his horse, and left in a rush.

It took longer to pick up the tracks this time, and he chafed as he searched for them. It was late morning before he did and he pushed on, hardly paying attention to the tracks. He didn't think they'd head for Wichita either, but he thought they would head around the city when they got near it. All the robberies they had had Van Horn do were north of Wichita, mostly to the northwest, so Coppersmith figured that's where they were heading.

Around midafternoon, he stopped alongside a small stream with a single cottonwood keeping sentinel. He hobbled the horse, loosened the cinch on the saddle and let the animal out to graze and drink. He drank from the stream himself, then lunched on a piece of ham he had brought with him from the restaurant. When he finished, he wandered around a little to stretch his legs. In so doing, he looked at the road a few feet from the stream and realized there were no tracks of his quarry.

"Dammit all to hell," he snapped. Quickly he tightened the cinch, removed the hobbles, mounted up, and rode back along the trail. He stopped every hundred yards or so to check, and with relief, finally picked up the trail, which had turned northwest. He followed as fast as he could to make sure he didn't lose the track again. But dark began to fall before long. And he pulled up for the night. There was no water, but there was grass nearby for the horse. He had a cold camp, finishing up the last of the ham and drinking from his canteen. He filled his hat from the canteen and let the horse drink, too.

In the morning, he had to be satisfied with some jerky and the last of the water in the canteen. Then he was in the saddle and moving on as rapidly as he could. With having had to search for the trail and follow it more slowly than he would have liked, it took him three days to reach Kingman. He started searching for the marshal, or even the county sheriff as Kingman was the seat of the same named county.

He found the marshal pretty easily but decided not to question him, at least not yet. To Coppersmith, the lawman looked rather shady. He did find the sheriff, who was no help, saying that he had been out of town for several days and did not know anything about those the bounty hunter was chasing. Coppersmith didn't entirely believe him but there was nothing he could do. Angrily he stomped to a boarding house, got a room, stabled the horse, and went to the first eatery he found. He crossly chowed down on chicken, sweet potatoes, and green beans, chewing as if the food was an enemy and he had to destroy it.

The meal did little to ease his temper, so he stalked though the town, hoping some of the anger would melt away with the exercise. Dark was falling when someone hissed at him from an alley, "Hey, mister."

With a hand on one of his Colts, Coppersmith stopped and peered into the shadows. "Who are you and what do you want?" he asked quietly.

"I have information about the men you're lookin' for."

"Well, come on out and talk to me."

"No, sir. If Marshal Jones or Sheriff Smith finds out I'm talkin' to you, I'll either be dead or wish I was."

"If this is a trap, you'll be dead for sure." Coppersmith looked around, saw that no one appeared to be paying attention, and slipped just inside the alley.

"Away from the street, mister, so no one can hear us."

"No, thanks."

"Take a pistol and stick it in my back. Or front if that'll make you feel better. I know this seems odd, but I'm afraid of those two fellas who called themselves lawmen."

"Turn around." When the man did, Coppersmith put the muzzle of a Colt against the man's lower spine. "March." Ten feet in, he said, "Stop. Turn around and lean against the wall." When the man did, the bounty hunter said, "All right, mister, talk to me."

"Those men you're followin', the ones with the little

girl, were through here a couple days ago. Well, not through, at least not at first."

"What the hell does that mean?"

"They stopped long enough to jaw with those two fake law dogs. I think they're among the men who run with those outlaws."

"What's the name of the leader of the outlaws?"

"Biddle. Bucky, I think."

"Seems you don't care for either the marshal or the sheriff. You doin' this to get back at them for some reason?"

"Partly. And I do have reason. I'm just a poor fella who mucks out stables and does other grimy jobs no one else wants to do. And they treat me as a nobody. I ain't much, but I am a man, even a poor, wretched one."

Coppersmith's teeth clenched. If the man was telling the truth, the bounty hunter knew just what he was feeling. Coppersmith had been treated the same way not too many years ago, until a man named Travis Van Horn had pulled him up out of that miserable existence.

"You said partly?"

"Yes. The other reason is the girl."

Coppersmith tensed. "What about her?"

"I was in Wichita maybe a year ago or a little less, takin' a bunch of hogs to the butcher there. Nobody else wanted to handle 'em for five or six days on the trail."

"They trusted you?"

"Sure. What else was I gonna do with a wagon load of hogs?"

"Nothin', but I imagine your bosses didn't just give them hogs to the butcher. He must've paid for 'em."

"He didn't give me any money. The butcher would pay when one of the farmers went to Wichita. I got paid when I got back to Kingman. If they decided they would." The last was said with a heavy dose of bitterness.

"So what has this got to do with the girl?"

"I was sittin' outside a general store eatin' a pickle when a couple came by with a little girl. Couldn't've been more than four of five. The parents ignored me, like most people do, but that little girl, she waved at me and said..." his voice cracked, "she said, 'Hello, sir.'" Her parents pulled her away, but I ain't ever forgot that."

"So the girl with these outlaws made you think of that friendly little girl in Wichita?"

"The girl with those outlaws *is* the girl from Wichita."

Coppersmith was startled. "You sure?"

"'Course I'm sure. Ain't no other little girl said something like that to me. Ain't no little girl even ever spoke to me 'til that one. You gotta get her away from those bastards, mister."

"I intend to soon's I can track 'em down. I don't reckon you know where they were headin', do you?"

"Not for certain, but I overheard 'em say they were plannin' to stop by the old Bannister place. That's a cabin along a little creek runs into Pawnee Creek."

Coppersmith slid the Colt away and stood thinking a bit, then asked, "Are the marshal and sheriff part of Buddle's gang?"

"I think so, but I ain't sure. If they ain't they protect them fellas whenever they're in this part of Kansas."

"You gonna be all right?"

"Reckon so. Nobody pays any real attention to me unless it's to make fun of me. I sleep in the stable with the mules, so I can get there no trouble unless someone sees me leavin' the alley. They won't though. I'll go that way."

Coppersmith was vaguely aware of the man's arm pointing to the end of the alley away from the street.

"How do I get to this Bannister place?"

"Five miles northwest of town there's a creek. Follow it west just a couple miles and you'll be there."

Coppersmith nodded, though the man could barely see it. Then he said, "I hope you know, mister, that if I learn you've been lyin' or are sendin' me into a trap, I'll come back and put a bullet in your head, don't you?"

"Yep. Don't matter, though. I ain't lyin'. I just want you to help that child."

"I'll do my best. Now, scoot—what's your name anyway?"

"Can't tell you that."

"All right, go on, get."

9

COPPERSMITH SAT ON THE BED IN HIS ROOM AT the shabby hotel and pondered his next move. Getting Lizette away from the outlaws was his priority. Traveling to Wichita would take him more than two days if he pushed it some, then another two-plus days back here. In that time, Biddle and his men might be long gone. He could send Marshal Dan Quinn a telegram, but if what the man in the alley had indicated, the lawmen were outlaws, or at least protective of them. And that meant they likely had their own man as telegrapher.

He could go after Biddle by himself, which didn't present much of a problem as far as confronting them, but that could endanger Lizette. It might be the only way, though, but he would have to give it more thought.

A more immediate issue was whether the marshal and the sheriff truly were close to the outlaws. If they were, getting Lizette out might be all the tougher if the two lawmen decided to make Coppersmith a wanted man. That would not help the situation at all.

Making it all the worse was that he had little time. He

could not sit here in Kingman wondering what to do or trying to get a fix on who the good men were and who were the bad. And he likely would never know.

He finally stretched out on his bed and tried to sleep. It did not come easily or quickly. He felt cranky in the morning and was in a foul mood at breakfast when the marshal, whose name he still didn't know, strolled up to his table.

"Thought you'd be headin' out after those folks first thing."

"And what's it to you whether I leave here in ten minutes or ten days?"

"You seemed rather anxious yesterday to meet up with those fellas. Any reason?"

"Whether I have a reason or not is none of your concern, Marshal."

"I could arrest you for mouthin' off to me, boy," the lawman snarled.

"Maybe you could, but you won't."

"And why is that?" the marshal asked smugly.

"Because you'd be dead before we got to the door of this restaurant."

"You think you're that good, eh?" the lawman asked with a chuckle.

"Yep. Would you like to test me?"

The marshal lost his smug look. "Ain't reason enough to. Yet. Just get out of my town within the next hour."

"Or what?"

"You'll see."

As foul a mood as Coppersmith was in, he considered just shooting the marshal, but his common sense stopped him. That would bring no end of trouble. He would do it without hesitation if he found out the marshal—or the sheriff, or both—were in cahoots with

Biddle, but just gunning down a lawman, even a bad one, in a restaurant would be folly. And it could endanger Lizette. But at least he knew now that she was alive, having learned it a few weeks ago now.

He left the eatery and stomped up the street to his hotel room, gathered his saddlebags and Winchester, and stomped to the livery stable. His horse was saddled.

"Why's my horse ready?" he asked, surprised.

"Sheriff Smith said to have it ready for you." Seeing the cloud of anger lingering in Coppersmith's eyes, he hastily added, "He said you wanted to get on the road soon, so it'd help if I did."

Coppersmith bit back a retort. "Well, I didn't tell him to do this, but that ain't your doin'. In fact, it saves me some time and effort. He handed the man five dollars. "Thanks," he muttered as he tied the saddlebags on and shoved the Winchester in the scabbard. Mounted, he nodded thanks and trotted out of the huge barn the liveryman ran.

Half a mile or so outside Kingman, Coppersmith looked over his shoulder for some reason and saw that he was being followed. The knowledge did not improve his humor. Since there was nowhere for him or his followers to hide, they all just rode on. The followers made no effort to catch up to him. They just hung back, following, and far enough so that he could not tell who they were, though he had was sure he knew. Coppersmith was a bit worried that once they got a little farther from the town, where there was less chance of anyone else being around, they might backshoot him from a distance. It made him ride with hunched shoulders, which only increased his annoyance.

Suddenly he had an idea. He came to a stop and dismounted. A glance told him the others had also stopped. Coppersmith rummaged around in one of his saddlebags and came up with a mirror he used for shaving on the trail. He climbed back into the saddle and rode on. Being careful not to let the sun hit the mirror, he used it to keep an eye on his followers, raising it every few minutes to check on them. If he saw that they were unlimbering their rifles, he would impress upon them that such activity was not done by civilized men. He grinned to himself. *Those two civilized?* he thought, breaking into a laugh.

He had been traveling northwest intending to head for the old Bannister place, but before long he decided that his followers needed to see the sights of the flat, treeless countryside, so he turned east. Half a mile on, he turned south, another half mile and he went east, then north after about the same distance, and near the same length, finally west.

An hour later, he came across good size creek lined with cottonwoods, willows, and various shrubs and bushes. He entered the water, then turned and galloped upstream. Before his followers could catch on that he was racing upstream in the creek, he pulled out on the southwest side and headed back the way he had come.

He could hear their voices and stopped. He dismounted, tied his horse to a branch, and stalked quietly forward. He halted when the voices were close. Standing behind a cottonwood, he peered out. As he had thought, it was Marshal Jones and Sheriff Smith.

He wondered what he should do. His inclination was to shoot the two lawmen, if they really were lawmen, and be done with it. But it was not in his nature to just shoot down two men wearing badges just for following him. They could be, he thought, just making sure he was leaving the area.

But he doubted that. He expected they would kill him soon if he allowed it. He figured they were just waiting for a place like this. But supposition was not surety. On the other hand, he could not just disarm them and let them ride back to Kingman. They would put out wanted papers on him, even if just for themselves, then get up a posse and come after him. His choices were rather grim —shoot them down or give them license to hunt him down.

"I don't like bein' followed by men who wish to do me harm," Coppersmith said from behind the tree.

"Who's that?" Jones asked, startled.

"You know damn well who it is. You been followin' me all mornin'. I don't like a couple of stinkweeds like you trailin' and aimin' to shoot me down whenever you feel like it. You want to shoot me dead Let's do it out in the open, me against you two."

"You're crazy, mister," Smith said. "We ain't followin' you and we don't mean you any harm."

"You two must be dumber than river rocks if you think I'm gonna believe such hogwash."

"You kill us, the people of Kingman and Kingman County will hunt you down."

"I don't know about the county, but the people in the city will like as not piss on your graves. Runnin' roughshod over people is no way to gain their affection."

"You're soundin' crazier every minute," Jones said. "Why don't you let us bring you back to Kingman and let Doc Cale see if he can help you regain your reason."

"I don't need a doctor. You won't either when I'm through with you. All you'll be needin' is the boneyard director." Coppersmith could tell by the voices that the two men were spreadin' apart, a good defensive move. But he was not worried.

"Look, mister, whatever your name is, we're gettin' tired of you and all this nonsense. Now come on out here and let us escort you back to Kingman to talk about things."

"Nothing to talk about, Sheriff. I've done nothing wrong. If you've been protectin' Biddle and his group of outlaws, like I've heard you are, then it's you who're doin' wrong. Aidin' men like Biddle is not a wise decision on your part."

Ten or fifteen feet separated the two men now, and Jones was still edging away.

With a sigh of annoyance, Coppersmith pulled a Colt and put a shot just to the left of Jones' left foot. "That's far enough, Marshal."

The man stopped and stood frozen.

"Now I've got a proposal for you two. You surrender to me and let me take you to Wichita where I'll turn you over to a federal marshal and he can decide what to do with you, which means you'll probably have to go to court. If it's shown you've been helpin' Biddle, it likely will be bad for you. But maybe you can convince a judge that you were just duped by the outlaw. You're dumb enough, a judge might even believe it. So, what'll it be, boys?"

"Ain't our way, boy," Smith said. "Now come on out and face us. At least you'll die like a man instead of some rabbit hidin' behind a tree."

As Coppersmith stepped out into the small clearing right on the stream's edge, he asked, "Whatever made you help Biddle and his outlaws?"

"Money," Jones said.

"And power," Hayes added.

"You think runnin' roughshod over a town lie

Kingman makes you powerful? Lordy, dumb ain't nearly strong enough a word to describe you two idiots."

"Watch your name-callin' boy," Smith said.

"Or what?" Coppersmith said with a laugh. "You gonna shoot me? I already offered you that. But you've been too fainthearted to take me up on that offer." His face hardened. "Time to make a decision, boys. Either you surrender and let me take you to Wichita or pull those pieces."

The two lawmen looked at each other, then both went for their revolvers.

Coppersmith, in no rush, still put two bullets into each man's chest before they could clear leather.

"Damn fools," the bounty hunter muttered as he checked each man. Both were dead.

He got his horse and tied it nearby, then rummaged through Smith's and Jones' saddlebags, finding nothing he could eat. "Reckon they didn't figure to be out here very long," he muttered.

He lifted each man and tossed the body over his saddle. He tied the reins of one to the saddle horn of the other, then mounted and, with the reins to the first horse in hand, trotted back toward Kingman. Just before the town limits, he untied the two horses, then sent them running toward Main Street with a strong smack on the rumps.

"Well, that was unpleasant," he said with a shake of the head. "All right, horse, we got some more ridin' to do." By noon he had reached the creek he sought, and then followed it along the line of cottonwoods and willows. In a couple hours, he spotted the cabin in something of a glade surrounded by trees. He quickly ducked back into the trees. He wished there was someplace with some height, so he could get a better look at the lay of the land, but like most of Kansas it was flat.

He was surprised to see only three horses in the makeshift corral made of thick logs. He had thought there'd be more men here. It was good, he thought, because it would mean smaller odds if a battle broke out. But it also made him wonder whether Lizette was here. If she were, and there were only three men guarding her, rescuing her would be a lot easier than if the whole gang were here.

He hobbled the horse and left it to graze while he kept an eye on the cabin. After an hour, he decided it was time to act.

10

COPPERSMITH WAITED AT THE EDGE OF THE cabin. After looking through a crack between the logs, he saw that Lizette was inside. He could, he thought, just burst in and take care of all three men before they even knew he was there. But he abandoned that idea right off. He was not going to do that with a five-year-old girl sitting right there to witness it all. No, he figured she had already endured more horrors than anyone should, let alone a child that young.

On the other hand, he had to get her out of there, and soon. Yet there seemed to be no other way, unless luck intervened. Moments later, it appeared that Lady Luck had been paying attention. One of the men stepped outside and headed toward the privy. Coppersmith was between the outlaw and the outhouse, so when the man reached the corner of the building, Coppersmith smashed him alongside the head with pistol barrel. As the man wobbled, the bounty hunter kicked him hard in the crotch. As the man bent at the waist in pain, Copper- smith grabbed his hair, pulled his head back, then jerked it forward, bringing his knee up at the same time. The man's face shattered, and he slumped to the ground, his mug a mishmash of blood, bone, and brain matter.

Coppersmith dragged the outlaw's body to the back of the house and dropped it there. "One down, two to go," he muttered as he returned to his position.

He was getting itchy again when he heard the door open.

"Edgar? Edgar, where the hell are you? You get lost in the privy?" There was a pause, then, "Don't be playin' a game, Edgar, damn you. 'Diah wants his supper, and it's your turn to man the cook stove."

Coppersmith heard the man start walking toward him, and a grim smile cross his lips. When the man reached the corner of the cabin, Coppersmith grabbed him, jerked him around, and shoved his twelve-inch Bowie up through the bottom of the man's chin up into his brain. He was dead before he hit the ground. The bounty hunter dragged that body off and dumped it near the first. "Odds are gettin' better, Jace," he said quietly to himself.

As Coppersmith had thought, it wasn't long before the third man came out, looking for the first two. "I don't want to have to come chasin' after you boys. Now get your asses back here."

Coppersmith worked up a healthy burp. A moment later the third man showed up at the corner of the cabin. When he did, the bounty hunter smacked him hard with a pistol barrel right between the eyes. The man wobbled, then sank to his knees, his eyes crossed as he weaved.

Coppersmith took the man's revolver, unloaded it, and tossed it away. Then he tied the outlaw's hands behind his back with the man's bandanna. Using his knife, Coppersmith cut off two pieces of the man's filthy trousers. He used one to tie the outlaw's feet together and shoved the other in the man's mouth. He rose. "That ought to keep you quiet for a bit," the bounty hunter murmured. Then aloud he said, "Don't go nowhere."

Coppersmith went into the house. Lizette was sitting on a cot playing with a rag doll. She was filthy and looked tired, hungry, and scared. "You all right, young lady?"

"I guess so," she mumbled, afraid to look up, but then she sneaked a peek she said, "Hey, I met you before when I was little. You were with that man whose name was Horn or something. You helped Mama and Papa and the others."

"All true, little miss. Travis Van Horn was—is—a friend of your parents." He almost choked on the words, wondering how someone, anyone, would find the words to tell this child that her parents—for that's what Emil and Anneliese Bassmyer were to Lizette—were dead.

"You hungry?"

Lizette clamped her little lips together, and Coppersmith had to force himself not to swear in front of the girl. It took even more willpower to keep from going outside this instant and teaching the outlaw that it wasn't nice to abuse five-year-old girls. He sighed. That would come soon enough.

"It's all right, Lizette. I ain't like those other men. I come to take you home. You're safe now."

The child's scared eyes betrayed her hunger though.

"There any food? I'm hungry, too."

"Chicken on the stove," Lizette whispered. "Edgar was gonna make taters but he went away."

"And he won't be comin' back. You can be sure of that. Like I said, you're safe now." He walked to the stove where some fried chicken rested in a frying pan. It was cold but it should be just as filling as if it were hot. He put some on a plate and set it on the table. "Well, come on, you best have some before I eat it all."

Still looking terrified, Lizette managed the smallest giggle, then tentatively went and sat at the table. She even more tentatively started eating.

"You like coffee?"

"Yes," the child answered in a whisper. "Very much."

Moments later there was a cup sitting before her on the table.

"All right, Lizette, I have to go outside and take care of some things." When he saw the fresh look of terror on the girl's face, he added, "Those bad men won't come back to hurt you anymore. I promise. I sent them all away. I just need to do a few things, then we'll ride on out of here and head home. You just eat and everything'll be all right."

He wondered where his authoritative kindness to children came from. This was just like Clay Dawes, the boy he had found in Texas whose parents had been killed by a vile outlaw gang led by a man named Brady Rutledge. It was hard to believe he could win a child's trust considering his own tormented childhood. He sighed. It didn't matter how he did it, only that he could, and did. He headed outside and around the corner of the building, where the outlaw waited, eyes bugged in rage.

"Comfortable?" Coppersmith asked, voice thick with sarcasm.

The outlaw mumbled something that could not be deciphered and certainly not understood because of the gag in his mouth.

"You seem to be talkative, which is a good thing since we are going to have a little discussion. I will ask a question, take the gag out of your mouth, and you will answer." Seeing the plotting going on it the man's eyes, the bounty hunter added, "Should you scream, or even try to, I will hurt you. Badly." The scheming fell from the outlaw's face.

"Now, the first question will be easy for you. What's your name?" He pulled the gag free.

It took a few moments for the man to gather up enough saliva to be able to talk. "Alex Battersby."

"Good start, Mr. Battersby. Where is Biddle?"

"I don't know." His eyes widened in fear when Coppersmith pulled his big knife. "I swear I don't know. He just left me and the others here a few days ago, tellin' us to watch over the girl."

"This the first time?"

"Nope. Every few weeks or so. Usually me, Edgar, and Slim, but sometimes it was others."

"When's he comin' back?"

"Don't know that either. Sometimes he's gone just a day or two, a few times almost a week."

"Did you degrade the girl?" Coppersmith's voice was edged in steel and as cold as death.

"Me? No, sir. I'll rob banks, raise hell in a town, shoot people, but I ain't one to touch a child that way."

The man's voice rang true, and Coppersmith believed him.

"Any of the others do so?"

"Not that I know of. If such a thing was done, it was done while I wasn't there. Anybody but Biddle was tryin' to do it, I would've stopped 'em."

"You're an honorable man, Mr. Battersby," Coppersmith spat. "Won't touch the girl in an obscene way but you let her live in filth and slowly starve to death."

"I... We..."

Coppersmith decided he would get no more information from Alex Battersby. He slapped a hand across the outlaw's mouth and plunged the Bowie hilt deep in Battersby's chest. In moments the man was dead. Coppersmith wiped the blade off on one of the man's sleeves, rose, and dragged the body to where the others were. He wondered how he could get the bodies back to Wichita so he could collect the reward without traumatizing the girl even more by having to ride alongside three corpses. Then he decided finding the girl alive and bringing her back to Wichita was reward enough.

Back inside the cabin, Lizette was still eating. She glanced up when Coppersmith entered the room, fear flashing across her face, but she relaxed when she saw who it was. He smiled at her. "You leave me any of that chicken or did you eat it all?" He almost pulled a Colt and shot himself when he saw the horror that jumped onto her countenance. "Lizette, Lizette, dear child, I was only joshin', really." *You're a damn fool, Jace Coppersmith*, he thought. "You can eat all the chicken in the cabin, in the whole world. Every chicken that ever was, you can eat it. You can go around the world, shoutin', 'Give me chicken,' and everybody would have to do it. You'd eat so much chicken you'd weigh more than my horse."

The terror faded after a few moments as the tale, even for a five-year-old, grew more outlandish. She ended up giggling.

He was hungry, he decided, so he grabbed the rest of the fried chicken and made short work of it.

"Well, young lady, are you ready to go home?" he asked as he sipped one more coffee.

"Yes, please."

"Can you ride a horse?"

"Mama wouldn't let me. She said I was too young, but I'm not." She was indignant.

"No, you're not," Coppersmith agreed. "Would you like to try?"

She sat in thought for a bit. "Would it be a small horse?"

"No, I'm afraid not, Lizette. You can ride with me if you want, though." He paused, a realization hitting him. "Is that how you moved around with those bad men?"

"Yes," she whispered, ashamed.

"There's nothing to be ashamed off. You had to do what they said. If it'd make you feel bad to ride in front of me, you could ride behind me. Might be uncomfortable, though."

"I don't know."

Coppersmith suddenly grinned. "I got something that might make it more fun if you ride in front of me."

"What?" Lizette asked eagerly.

"It'll be a surprise." Seeing darkness creeping over her face, he said, "A good surprise."

"All right." She sounded half happy, half fearful.

"Then let's go."

"Where's your horse?" the girl asked when they stepped outside, confused.

"In those trees over there," he said, pointing, thankful that the bodies were on the opposite side of the house from where the horse was.

"Why'd you leave him there?"

"There was water and lots of grass for him to eat."

"That's good," Lizette said seriously.

"Pard—that's his name—would agree." He paused. "Can I carry you?"

"No, I'll walk."

"All right."

"But you can hold my hand," she said shyly.

"Well, I'll be honored to do that, Miss Lizette."

Before long they were riding off, Lizette perched between Coppersmith and the saddle horn.

"When're you gonna show me that surprise?" the girl asked barely minutes after they had left.

"Soon's we get a little farther."

Out on the flats, leaving behind the trees lining the stream, Coppersmith took Lizette's hands and put the reins in them. "Here you go, miss, you have control of the horse."

"I do?"

"Yep." He took her small hands in his big, hard ones and tugged on the reins to guide her. "Do you now left from right?"

"Yes."

"All right, if you want the horse to go left, you use the reins to pull his head to the left. If you want to go to the right, you pull him the other way. Gently, though."

They did not spend long on the trail that afternoon. Coppersmith had mostly wanted to get Lizette away from the cabin. So they made camp before long. Lizette was helpful, and Coppersmith was glad the weather was nice. That way he could let her have the bedroll while he slept without coverings.

The girl's lessons began again the next day. She proved to be a quick study, and by afternoon of the second day on the trail, she was controlling the animal as if she had been doing so for years. With his help, which she didn't realize.

11

FIVE DAYS LATER THEY RODE INTO WICHITA.
Word quickly spread and people began lining the streets.
Marshal Dan Quinn and Deputy Harry Wallace ran up.

"How? Where? What?" Quinn said, trying to make a
coherent sentence.

"Later, Dan."

"Where's Mama and Papa?" Lizette asked, looking
around wide-eyed at the growing crowd.

"They're—" Wallace started, but he stopped in a
hurry when he saw the look in Coppersmith's eyes. It
was the look of death. His.

"Go on out to the farms, Harry," Quinn said. Warn
'em what to expect." He looked up at Lizette and smiled.
"You'll stay with me and my family, Lizette, 'til some of
your folks can get here."

"All right."

Coppersmith waved his hand around. "Need to
avoid... trouble, Dan," he said. "Can't have someone
yellin' something about..."

"I know," the marshal said with a nod. He called

another deputy, Max Bramwell, over to him. "Head on over to my house and let Edith know that Lizette will be arrivin' soon. I'll explain to her later. She—and you—are to say nothing to this girl other than pleasantries."

"Yes, sir." Bramwell headed off.

"Go on, Jace," Quinn said. "I'll take care of the crowd."

"All right, Lizette, let's ride to the marshal's house. Just past the bakery, you turn right, two blocks up you turn left, then right again. Can you do that?"

"Yes." She was offended that her abilities were being questioned.

Coppersmith smiled over the girl's head as they moved off. Quinn was already shouting for people to move on.

FIFTEEN MINUTES LATER, Coppersmith strolled into Quinn's office. The marshal was sitting at his desk; Wallace and Bramwell leaned against walls. The bounty hunter did the same next to the door. "What now?" he asked.

"I go home and talk to Edith. Harry and Max will keep everyone from town away from her. Then we wait 'til some of the Germans turn up. It'll be their job to talk to Lizette. How they handle it is up to them."

Coppersmith nodded. "Where's Travis and Reese?"

"Ain't sure. Travis went off on his own like usual these days. Reese was still out checking towns like you were doin'."

"Any way to get a hold of 'em?"

Quinn shrugged. "Soon's I leave here, I'm gonna head

to the telegrapher's and have him send out wires to every town within a fifty-mile radius."

"What're you gonna say in 'em?"

"I aim to keep it short, something like 'Get home. Lizette's here.'"

"Sounds about right."

"You look beat, Jace," Wallace said. "Was it bad?"

Coppersmith shrugged. "Not as bad as it could've been. I just wanted to make sure Lizette didn't see too much horribleness after all she'd been through. Finally managed." He related what had happened, keeping it brief.

"You're a hero to that girl, Jace," Quinn said as he rose.

"I ain't—"

"Don't be too humble. You saved that girl from a real hard time."

"I reckon."

"She was treated poorly. Maybe not as badly as we feared. Doesn't matter, though. We all saw how dirty and exhausted she was even though I reckon you made sure she was well fed as much as possible on the trail and made sure she got plenty of sleep. But even if they treated her well, it was horrible for that little girl just bein' taken from her parents and held away from them for a few months. Not to say whether she knew what happened to 'em."

"Doesn't she? How could she not know?"

"From what we figure, she was playin' in the yard when Biddle and his scum rode up. One of 'em grabbed her and rode off. She screamed, and that brought the Bassmyers out of the house. It was near suppertime, so Emil was home. Rest of the family was out in the fields still, or on their way home. That's when they were killed.

But by then Lizette was far enough away. And, of course, she was cryin' and scared and all. She never knew, we don't think." Quinn put his hand on the doorknob. "Now go get yourself cleaned up, get some grub, and get some sleep. Anything happens, one of us'll come and get you."

"What if the Germans arrive? Won't take 'em long to get here."

"They'll need to deal with Lizette and how to explain that her parents are dead. They don't need you, me, or anyone else bein' around when they do so. Now, go do what I said." He pulled the door open and hurried out.

Moments later, Coppersmith followed him out. He left his horse at the livery stable, then had a meal at Fleming's. He decided a bath and new clothes were in order, so he bought a fresh outfit, went to Wheeler's tonsorial parlor, bathed, had his hair trimmed a little, and had a shave. Finally, he took a room at the Parker House. None of which he had to pay for. He was in his room, looking out the window when three wagons of Germans arrived, their horses lathered. He watched for a while as the Germans went to Marshal Quinn's. Wondering what the people were telling Lizette, he climbed into bed, thankful for a soft mattress and clean sheets.

A knock on the door woke Coppersmith. He rolled out of bed, grabbing a pistol as he did. He stood to the side of the door and opened it. "Herr Coppersmith?"

"Mr. Mueller?"

"Yah."

"Come in, then. When the man did, followed by his wife, Ingrid, Coppersmith took a quick look outside. There was no one else outside. He closed the door. Mueller said nothing about it.

"Sit, Mr. Mueller, Mrs. Mueller." He pointed to the two plush chairs that flanked a small table. He perched on the bed. "Have you told Lizette?" he asked.

"Yah."

"How is she handlin' it?"

"As vell as can be expected. She is young and doesn't completely understand."

Coppersmith nodded, then asked, "What can I do for you, Mr. Mueller."

"Call me, Joachim, please. There is nothing you can do, Herr Coppersmith."

"Call me Jace."

Mueller's head bobbed in acknowledgement. "You haf done much, so very much for us by bringing our dear Lizette back to us safe, if not unharmed."

"Was she...?"

"Ve don't t'ink zo. Though she has been mistreated, of course, as you no doubt realized."

"What'll happen to her now?"

"Ve are not sure. Frau Mueller and I are prepared to take her in and consider her another of our children. Ve vere close to Emil and Anneliese, so Lizette knows us vell. But ve must talk vith Herr Van Horn."

"That would be appropriate. I imagine he'll allow Lizette to stay with you. Like last time, I'm sure he won't think himself a good candidate for raisin' a child."

"I hope you don't t'ink poorly of me, Jace, but ve hope that is the case. Ve t'ink the girl vill be better off vith us."

"I think you're right, and I'm pretty sure he'll agree. I'll talk to him if you think it's necessary, but like I said, I expect he'll agree with you."

"*Danke*. Vell, ve must be going. Again, I must offer

many thanks for you rescuing Lizette from those *Bösewichte*—villains."

"It was my pleasure to do so. I just wish I could've done it sooner."

"Better late than never, I hear is a saying." Mueller hesitated. "Vill ve be bothered by these men?"

"Not by the three who were holdin' Lizette when I found her. They won't be botherin' anyone ever again. The leader and several other of his men are still out there. I'll be searchin' for 'em within the next couple days. I'm waitin' to see if Travis or a friend of ours who was helpin' us show up. Meanwhile, I'll have some folks watch over you."

"*Danke*. Come, *Liebling*." He held out his hand, and his wife took it and rose. "*Auf Wiedersehen*, Herr Coppersmith. I hope vhen ve see you again, it vill be better times."

"Me, too, Mr. Mueller, ah, Joachim."

The next morning, from his window, Coppersmith watched as the Muellers, with Lisette in their wagon, the Fasebinder family, and the Jaegers rode out of town. He could not help but feel a slight tug of loss as the wagon in which Lizette rode faded.

He finally left his room and headed to McSween's restaurant, where he desultorily ate what should have been a fine meal. Then he roamed around town for a bit, until he got tired of the many people who practically fawned over him for rescuing Lisette. After a short while, he could stand it no longer, so he went back to his room, where he spent much of the rest of the day cleaning his pistols and reading the newspaper.

He ate supper with the Quinns. The marshal had seen the people flattering Coppersmith and knew the bounty hunter would not like it, so he invited the young man to his home. It was somewhat uncomfortable, but Coppersmith relaxed considerably.

——

COPPERSMITH AND QUINN were just finishing breakfast at McSween's the next morning when they heard a commotion. The two walked outside in time to see Reese Milstead pulling up his horse in front of the marshal's office. Milstead dismounted and hurried into the building.

"Reckon you better go talk to him, Dan," Coppersmith said.

"Harry's there. He can do it." Then Quinn sighed. "But I guess it's my job, so I ought to go see to it. Want to join me?"

"Not a chance. I think I'll go check on my horse and try to avoid some of our fine citizens, though I am glad they're startin' to leave me alone."

After lunch, Coppersmith wandered to Quinn's office. The marshal was sitting there, feet up on the desk. "I ain't interruptin' some serious law business am I, Dan?" the bounty hunter asked.

"I'd have to say yes you are. I just can't think of what it is right at the moment. Sit." When Coppersmith did, Quinn asked, "What're you doin' here, Jace?"

"I get on your bad side all of a sudden?"

"Hell, no. I didn't mean it in a bad way. Just poor phrasin' in askin' what I can do for you."

"You seen Reese since this mornin'?"

"Nope. Maybe you just missed each other at the stables."

"Reckon so. I—"

The door burst open and Milstead walked in and

glanced around. "Well, there you are, Jace. I've been lookin' for you."

"Well, now you found me." Coppersmith hadn't liked Milstead's tone.

"Don't you condescend to me, boy," Milstead snapped.

Coppersmith sat up a little straighter. "What'n hell're you talkin' about, Reese? All I said was you found me."

"Yeah, sure. The big hero talks down to the man who was goin' all over the countryside lookin' for his kin."

Coppersmith's eyes and voice grew cold. "You're angry because I found that little girl?" he asked, surprised. "Because she's not my kin? Hell, you don't even know her, never even seen her. Are you fool enough to think I'd crow about such a thing to you, or anybody else? Damn, you're even stupider than I thought."

"Why you—"

"Stop it, Reese," Quinn roared. When Milstead looked angrily at him, Quinn said, "Would you rather have had that little girl suffer for another day, week, months maybe before you found her simply because she's your niece? Maybe Jace's right, you're dumber than a bag of oats."

"But the people are all talkin' about what a damn hero he is. Think he's a saint or something."

"Have you ever known Jace to be such a braggart that he'd crow about himself that way? Do you see him sittin' here or wanderin' around town talkin' about what a big shot he is for rescuin' that girl? No, he's been embarrassed as all get out with people fawnin' over him. He's been reluctant to even show his face in public. If I was you, I'd be thankin' this man for what he did. He'd do the same if you had found Lizette."

"Well, hell, I gotta say I ain't dumber than a bag of

oats. I'm even dumber than that if such a thing can be true." He sighed. "I'm sorry, Jace. You know me, a damn hothead. I was so worried about Lizette and when I heard people crowin' about you, I figured you were tryin' to be a big shot around here."

"You should've known better, Reese."

"Yes, I should have. How is she?"

"She was tired, filthy, still scared when I saw her last." At Milstead's questioning look, he added, "I took her to Dan's house where Edith cared for her 'til the Germans came. Joachim Mueller said he planned to take her home where he and Ingrid would raise her as their own."

"What about Travis?"

"You know damn well he wouldn't be a good father. He knows it, too. At least he always has. But Mueller said he would talk to Travis to make sure the arrangement was all right with him.

"It will be, I'm sure."

12

TRAVIS VAN HORN ROARED INTO WICHITA, scattering people, horses, dogs, or anything foolish enough to get in his way. He slammed to a stop in front of Marshal Dan Quinn's office and, without even hitching his mount, charged inside.

"Where is she?" he bellowed.

"Good afternoon, Travis. Hope you've had an agreeable journey."

"Where is she?" he demanded, voice even louder.

"Pleasant weather we're havin', wouldn't you say?"

Van Horn's eyes bulged with anger. "Where is she, dammit?"

"And who might you be inquiring about?" Quinn's voice was still calm and measured.

Van Horn looked as if a blood vessel in his neck would burst. He started to walk angrily toward Quinn.

"Don't, Travis," Coppersmith said from his place leaning against the wall in a corner. He had a cocked revolver in his hand.

"You're not gonna shoot me, Jace," Van Horn said confidently.

"You keep actin' like an ass and I certainly will. Now shut your trap and sit. Maybe if you act like a rational fella, you might get an answer."

Barely choking back his anger, Van Horn did so. "Where's Lizette?" he asked in a tight but polite voice.

"With the Germans," Quinn said. "Specifically, the Muellers. They're plannin' on takin' her in and raisin' her."

"Like hell. I ain't gonna permit it."

Reese Milstead walked in just as Coppersmith said, "You really can't help but act like an ass, can you?" He decided the risk was not great, uncocked his six-gun, and dropped it into the holster.

"You're just findin' that out?" Milstead asked with a grin. Then he saw the serious faces around him. "What's goin' on, boys?"

"This addle-brained galoot came chargin' in here like a ravin' madman, demandin' to know where Lizette was. I told him, then told him what the Muellers said about takin' her in and he started gettin' even more *loco*."

"Reckon me and my brother are more alike in temperament that is good for folks. What did he propose?"

"Nothin'. Didn't have a chance to, but from how angry he was I figure he was gonna say that he was takin' her to... well, who the hell knows."

"One thing we do know," Coppersmith threw in, "is that he ain't fit to be a father to a young girl."

"That's a fact," Milstead said.

"To hell with all of you. I'm gonna fetch my daughter." He started to rise.

"Sit!" Milstead ordered. "Use your head for once, ya damn fool. What're you gonna do with her? You gonna settle down and be a farmer like the Germans? Be a clerk in Slater's mercantile? Or maybe you plan to just take her along when you ride down into the Nations chasin' scum like you been doin' for maybe a hundred years now."

"Well, no, I ain't gonna do that. But I reckon I can find something that's respectable and allow me to make a good life for Lizette."

Milstead, Coppersmith, and Quinn all shook their head.

"Now, stop and think, Travis," Coppersmith said, "for as long as you need to. A minute ought to be enough. Does any of what you're thinkin' of doin' make any sense?"

"Well, no," Van Horn mumbled. "But I—"

"How long you been a bounty hunter, Travis?" Milstead asked. "Seriously."

"I don't know, ten years, maybe a few years more."

"And you expect you'll just find another way of makin' a livin' that'd let you raise a little girl?"

"I reckon I can," Van Horn said defensively.

"Like what?" Coppersmith asked. "We've already ruled out farmin' and clerkin'. Maybe be a baker? Or a butcher?"

"Maybe a gunsmith," he mumbled.

"Travis, you know how to shoot guns, not fix 'em," Milstead snapped.

"Face it, Travis," Coppersmith said, "you ain't cut out to be a father, especially not for a little girl. You knew that last time you were out there and saw Lizette—for the first and only time. Nothing's changed."

"She's lost three parents—four if you count me,

which no one should—she shouldn't face losin' others, especially her father."

"She doesn't know you're her father. If she even remembers you from the last time you were here, she'll remember you as a friend of her parents, which Emil and Anneliese were in every sense of the word. You'd be just another hard-lookin' man carryin' guns," Coppersmith said.

"Just like the ones who killed the Bassmyers and took her away," Milstead added.

Van Horn looked defeated, a man suddenly worn down by the mistakes he had made in life, the good things he had missed. "What am I gonna do?" he asked, trying to keep the anguish out of his voice.

"Go talk to the Muellers. Joachim said he and Ingrid wouldn't do anything except be caretakers of Lizette 'til they talked to you," Quinn said. "They figured you'd know you weren't in any position to be a father, but they didn't want to presume anything. So, they wanted to talk to you in the hope that you would have no objection to them takin' Lizette in."

Van Horn shook his head. "Looks like I'm the only fool here," he said with a sigh.

"Nope, not by a long shot, brother," Milstead said.

Van Horn looked at him and smiled a little. "Made a fool of yourself again, too, eh?"

"As I do too often."

Van Horn nodded and turned back to face Quinn. I'll clean myself up—don't want to frighten that girl too much—then head—" He stopped, brow furrowed in thought. "How'd she get here, anyway?" he asked.

"Jace brought her in," Quinn said. "Rescued her. Near about a week ago, that right, Jace?"

Coppersmith nodded.

Van Horn swung around on his chair. "How? What?"

"Don't think I'm capable?" Coppersmith responded in a tight voice.

"Of course I think you're capable. Wondered how you found her and what you needed to do to get her out."

"Traveled around several towns. In a couple I heard about a small group of men travelin' with a little girl. I wasn't sure if it'd be them because I thought there'd be more."

"We did think that if they did this, they might leave some men out of town so as not to raise suspicions," Milstead said.

"That's what I figured. If I was wrong, well, it just meant more searchin'. I tracked 'em to a place called Milton, then Kingman, couple three days' ride west of here. The town marshal and county sheriff were in cahoots with Biddle and thought to ambush me when I headed out to the outlaws' hideout."

"You're here, so I figure they ain't?" Milstead said.

"That's a fact. Put both of 'em down. I don't think they were well liked in the area so I ain't worried about somebody chasin' me for their killin's. Anyway, I found the cabin that a concerned citizen, a poor fella much like I was, though older than when Travis pulled me out of that wretched town, told me was a hideout Biddle sometimes used. An old farmhouse. I watched it for a spell and figured there were three men. Wasn't sure the girl was there until I snuck up and saw her through a crack in the logs where the chinkin' had fallen out."

"So you busted in and started blazin' away like you've done before. Shot 'em all dead and walked off with Lizette," Milstead said almost happily.

The other three men looked at him as if he were insane.

"Ah, no, Reese. I figured that little girl had gone through enough already without me blastin' away and killin' three men right in front of her."

"See, Travis, like I said, you ain't the only idiot in the family."

"So I took 'em out one by one." He grinned crookedly. "First one come out to use the privy, and I got him. Second come out lookin' for him and I took him out. The third one came out lookin' for the other two. That was the end of that."

Silence descended but lasted only a few moments before Van Horn said, "Thank you, Jace. Not only for savin' Lizette but also doin' it in a way that wouldn't hurt her mind any more than you needed to. Many men, includin' me—"

"And me," Milstead threw in.

"—would not have that much sense and decency."

Coppersmith shrugged, embarrassed by the accolades.

"How much was the reward?" Van Horn asked.

"I never thought to ask that," Milstead said.

A flash of anger crossed Coppersmith's face. "Didn't get any." When the two other bounty hunters looked at him in surprise, he added, "I didn't think it a good idea to spend five days or so on the trail with a five-year-old girl who'd been traumatized for a few months cartin' along three dead bodies that were gettin' riper by the day."

"Jesus, Travis, I'm glad it wasn't you or me found that girl. Lord knows how bad off she'd be under our care for some days on the trail."

Van Horn nodded. "Like I said, Jace, you're a sensible and decent man, and I'm glad to know you." He rose and stuck out his hand.

"Ah, hell, Travis, this ain't necessary."

"Yes, it is."

Milstead, then Quinn also offered respectful handshakes.

"Now can we talk about something else?" Coppersmith said.

"Like what?" Quinn asked.

"Anything. I don't give a damn. Just as long as it ain't about me."

Silence again came over then until Van Horn said, "Well I better be gettin' out to the Muellers' place."

"Tomorrow's soon enough, Travis," Quinn said.

"But it's been, what, almost a week since Lizette got back?"

"About that, yep," Quinn said. "But another day won't matter any. Get yourself cleaned up, have a couple good meals, and get some rest. I'd think you were ridin' pretty hard and long to get back here."

"I was, that's true." He rubbed a hand across his face. "I didn't know how tired I was 'til you mentioned sleep."

"Didn't take much to figure it. By the way, where'd you hear about Lizette?"

"Medicine Lodge. I've been reluctant to stop in towns for obvious reasons, but I was short on just about everything, so I thought I'd take the risk. I was just comin' out of a general store when I saw a poster saying a little girl had been found. Couldn't get on my horse fast enough. Took me two days of hard ridin', but it was worth it."

"If you had been in Medicine Lodge a few weeks ago, you might've found Lizette then. I went through there a couple weeks ago.

"Damn." Van Horn sighed and shook his head. Finally, he said, "Speakin' of me not goin' into towns, I need you to try and quash any paper that's out on me,

Dan. Every place I robbed likely has a handbill out on me."

"I'll do what I can. Ain't gonna be easy. These towns aren't happy with bein' robbed—what a surprise, eh. But I know some of the lawmen out in those places. Hopefully they'll agree once I tell 'em the reason. I should be able to get it cleared up. Might take a little while though. Try and keep out of trouble in the meantime."

"Ain't likely," Coppersmith said.

"Meanwhile, what're you boys gonna do after Travis talks to the Muellers?"

"Get Biddle," all three bounty hunters said in unison.

"I hope like hell you do. But you couldn't run him down before."

"We were afraid of steppin' on toes, endangerin' Lizette's life," Coppersmith said. "That is no longer a restriction," Milstead said.

Quinn nodded.

"One thing, though, Marshal. I know it ain't your jurisdiction, but I'd be obliged if you were to keep an eye on the Germans, the Muellers especially."

"You afraid they'll do something wrong?"

"Nope. I'm afraid Biddle will come after them if he hears Lizette is there."

"I'll have someone out there all the time as soon as you boys ride off. Sheriff Cartwright will help, too, I'm sure."

"Thanks, Dan."

"No need for thanks. And if you boys need anything for your hunt, just ask. If it's in my power, you'll get it."

The three bounty hunters nodded and filed out.

13

THE THREE HARD-LOOKING MEN STOPPED IN front of the Mueller house and dismounted. Joachim and Ingrid Mueller came out of the house onto the porch, little Lizette between them. The Muellers' other children were bunched up behind them.

Before any of the adults could say anything, Lizette piped up, "Hello, Mr. Jace." She smiled glowingly.

"Me? I don't know you, do I, miss?"

The child looked confused. "Yes, we rode together after you took me away from those bad men."

"That's you? Well, how about that. I didn't even recognize you with you being all shined up like a bright new penny."

Lizette giggled

"See." Coppersmith pulled a new penny out of a pocket, walked up and handed it to the girl. "All bright and shiny, just like you." The bounty hunter looked up. Ingrid Mueller was smiling; her husband looked like he didn't know whether to be angry or happy.

Finished looking at the penny, Lisette glanced

around. Her eyes widened as little when she saw Van Horn. "I know you, too. You were here when Mama and—"

"Come, child," Ingrid said hastily and with authority, though there was caring in her voice. She herded Lizette and the other children inside.

"Damn, I knew I should never have come out here. Now I've set that little girl up for more pain."

"I don't mean to be callus, Herr Van Horn, but she vill haf to get used to her parents being gone. It is a hard truth for anyone, especially children, but that is the vay of life."

"Reckon you're right." Van Horn shuffled his feet a little, knowing what he wanted to say but unsure how to say it. Then he just decided to plunge ahead. "I'm mighty obliged, Mr. Mueller, for you and Mrs. Mueller to take Lizette in."

"It is our pleasure. Ve haf five children already and all are dear to us. Another bright young child vill be a blessing. And ve owe the Bassmyers so much. They vere good people."

"Yes, they were, Joachim. And again, I'm glad to know Lizette will have a good home, as she did with the Bassmyers." He shook his head. "I had entertained the thought of maybe bein' a real father to her." He hung his head in shame, then raised it to look at Mueller. "'Course, that was a damn fool idea. It took these two to make me realize that." He smiled ruefully. "I'm just glad they did so without havin' to thump me."

"Even as tough as they look, they vould have their hands full."

"Reckon they would but I'm damn sure I never want to find out." He paused as Ingrid came out on the porch again. Her husband looked at her.

"The other children vill take care of her. Don't vorry. It vill be all right."

Mueller nodded.

"Well, we best be goin', Joachim, Ingrid. Again, I'm mighty grateful for you takin' in Lizette."

"It is our pleasure, Travis. You are velcome here any time. You, too, Jace and... Just who is this other fellow?"

"My brother, Reese."

"Vell, ve don't know you, Reese, but if you are brother of this man, you are velcome to our house any time, too."

"I'm honored, sir."

Van Horn and Milstead mounted, but Coppersmith walked up to the porch and handed something to Ingrid. She looked down, then back at him. The bounty hunter smiled. "Pennies for the rest of the children. So they won't feel left out. None is new, though. That makes Lizette stand out a little, and I think she deserves that right now. Still, they all deserve a penny." He turned and mounted his horse.

Ingrid nodded and offered a soft smile.

"You know all the deputies in Wichita, Joachim? County ones, too?" Van Horn asked. When Mueller nodded, he added, "One or another of 'em will be out here from time to time to keep an eye on things. We don't think they'll be trouble but until we run those murderous, baby-stealin' bastards— Sorry ma'am."

"No need to be. They should be called vorse."

"You vill catch them though, yes?" Mueller asked.

"The devil will be shovelin' mountains of snow before I—any of us three—will quit 'til we run down those bastards." He smiled a little at Ingrid, who nodded.

They turned their horses and trotted off. A hundred yards away, Van Horn stopped and looked back over his shoulder. Coppersmith and Milstead stopped, too, and looked at each other. They knew they had seen Van Horn's misty eyes but were not about to say anything.

"Come on, dammit, let's ride," Van Horn suddenly snapped and galloped off.

———

"WHERE WE GONNA START, TRAVIS?" Milstead asked as they were waiting for a mule to be loaded with supplies.

"Ain't sure. Jace?"

"Kingman, I reckon. I found Lizette in a cabin not far from there. Don't know which way we'll head after that. It's been about two weeks since I found Lizette. No tellin' how long it took Biddle to get back there ready to pick up his men and the girl. He could be there now, or he could've shown up five minutes after I rode out."

"You're a bundle of hope, ain't you?"

"Just want you to be realistic, Travis. It might be months before we run those scum down."

"We can hope not," Milstead said.

"It won't," Van Horn said flatly, then called to the stable worker, "You gonna take all day to load that mule, boy?"

"Almost done, mister."

Less than five minutes later, the three men were leaving Wichita. They rode abreast, Coppersmith, the youngest, towing the pack mule. They were more than halfway to Kingman when they made camp, but Van Horn was not happy.

"Should've left sooner," he snapped as he paced the campsite waiting for supper to be done.

"Yep, should've," Milstead sarcastically. "Like yesterday or last week, or maybe last month."

"Don't be so sarcastic, Reese, dammit."

"Then don't be an ass, Travis. Sit down, eat. Food's almost ready. And keep your trap shut except to eat."

"But—"

"But what?

Van Horn sat and moodily ate.

————

THEY LEARNED NOTHING IN KINGMAN, other than that the two lawmen were not missed. As he was riding out of town, Coppersmith looked over and saw a disheveled, grimy man who looked nervously, expectantly at him. The bounty hunter nodded and smiled, and the man beamed.

The searchers turned south, then east. They been through Harper, Wellington, South Haven and were approaching Winfield.

"You want anything from town, Travis?" Milstead asked as they made a camp in a small stretch of trees along a stream a few miles outside town.

"Yeah, I want to go *in* the town, not sit out here like I've been doin'."

"For the maybe thousandth time we've told you, Travis, we can't risk havin' you ride into a town. We can't be sure Dan has gotten any paper out on you canceled. With that hair of ours you're easy to pick out. It's why, as you well know, I've kept shavin' mine off so I don't get mistaken for you. All we need is some damn marshal in some pissant little town arrestin' you because he saw a wanted poster on you that hasn't been withdrawn yet."

"And then," Coppersmith put in, "we'd have to try to

rescue you—if they haven't arrested us, too, for keepin' company with that dangerous fugitive from the law Travis Van Horn."

"And if we have to try to break you out of whatever jail that town has," Milstead said, jumping back into the one-sided conversation, "somebody likely would get hurt, maybe even killed. Could be one of us, could be a townsman, in which case they'll try to arrest me and Jace either as killers or accomplices to a killer."

"So," Coppersmith said, hoping to put an end to this, "you get to stay here and watch over the mule."

"But, dammit, I've been sittin' outside of every town we've been to. I'm plumb tired of it."

"You want to go ridin' into a town to test your luck, you can do so without me."

"Or me," Coppersmith noted.

"Dammit, for once I'd like to be the one who gets some information about Biddle's whereabouts myself so I can hunt down the man who took my daughter."

"I didn't want to say this before when you talked about Lizette, and I really don't want to do it now," Milstead said. "But it needs to be done." He paused, then said, "She ain't your daughter, Travis, not by any means other than you planted your seed in Gretchen."

"Why you son of a—"

"Sit down!" Coppersmith snapped.

"Or what?"

"Or I'll knock you down and sit on you 'til you regain your sense, if you ever do."

"Mighty cocky for some punk kid."

Coppersmith's eyes blazed red. "If I'm a punk you are, too, Travis," he said angrily. "You were the one who taught me just about everything. I've often told people that you not only turned me into a man hunter, you turned me into a man. Maybe I was wrong about you teachin' me that. Maybe I just learned it on my own."

"It's a worthy thing you're doin' in tryin' to hunt down Biddle for what he did. It's why Jace and I are right here with you. She ain't our child, either. But Jace knew the Bassmyers and from what he—and you—have told me, they were fine people, good, hard-workin', God-fearin' people trying to make a good life, ones worth callin' friends. It's worth huntin' down the men who killed 'em. But tryin' to make this about a child you don't know, who you've seen only twice for maybe five minutes each time, is wrong, Travis, just plain wrong."

"Think about it this way, Travis," Coppersmith said. "Suppose Biddle had killed the Muellers and took one of their young children, say four-year-old Elspeth. Wouldn't you be just as eager to hunt down Biddle as you are now about Lizette?"

"No," Van Horn said flatly. "Elspeth ain't my daughter. Lisette is."

Coppersmith sighed. "I give up, Reese. The man ain't just hardheaded, he's iron headed. There's no talkin' to him. He won't listen to anything that makes sense. He's got his mind made up that he's this wondrous pa to that little girl and he wants to kill Biddle to prove it. Or he thinks it'll prove it."

"You could be right, Jace. I think it's more than that, though. I think he's feelin' poorly about not bein' there when Lizette was born, and not bein' a real pa to her. I reckon that's been eatin' at him, and he thinks he can make up for that by killin' Biddle. It's why he was angry at you when he learned that you'd rescued Lizette. He wanted to be the one to do that. It'd prove he was a good father."

"You boys are plumb crazy," Van Horn growled.

Coppersmith rose. "Well, I'm goin' into town. Might even have a couple of snorts, which I haven't done in a while. Then in the mornin', I aim to ride out followin' any trail I can find of those scum. Reese, you're welcome to ride alongside me. Travis, you can go to hell. I'll even make sure you got a good horse for the ride. But you ain't comin' with me."

"Oh, sure, you probably got some idea of where they are and you're gonna go get 'em for the reward."

Milstead gasped as Coppersmith froze. "You're just lucky, Travis, that you're a friend. Well, used to be a friend. I don't know what the hell you are now. If you hadn't been my teacher, I'd kill you right this minute here and now."

"Think you could do that?" Van Horn sneered. The sneer dropped in a hurry when he found himself facing a cocked Colt .44 in Coppersmith's hand.

"Yes."

COPPERSMITH POINTED the muzzle to the sky, uncocked the weapon and holstered it again. "Don't ever come near me again, Travis, not unless you want to see which one of us is better with a six-gun."

"That day will come soon, boy."

"Just make sure you have the stones to come at me face to face rather than tryin' to shoot me in the back or while I'm sleepin'."

"You can count on it."

14

COPPERSMITH STARTED TO WALK AWAY BUT stopped at Milstead's voice. "Will you boys listen to yourselves? What in hell's gotten into the both of you? I've never seen two crazier men in all my life, and I've seen some mighty damn crazy ones. You sound like two schoolboys fightin' to see who can sit next to that cute pigtailed girl at school. You're disgustin'. I might not even wait 'til mornin'. I'm thinkin' I'll just ride out now and leave you two to kill each other if you think that'll solve the problem of findin' and killin' Biddle." He paused. "Oh, and Travis, about the reward. You say something like that again, Jace won't have to kill you. I will have already done so. Now that I know what kind of folks the Bassmyers were and what a darlin' little girl Lizette is, I'd go after Biddle even if I had to *pay* the reward on the bastard. I reckon Jace feels the same."

"I do."

Despite their threats, both Coppersmith and Milstead rode into town, asked questions, listened in on some conversations at a couple of saloons, bought a few supplies, and went back to their camp. Van Horn was asleep.

"Was I drunk last night?" Van Horn asked as he sat by the fire in the morning and reached for a mug to pour himself some coffee.

"Nope. Just stupid," Milstead said. "In fact, come to think of it, if you had been stupid, you would have made more sense than you did."

Breakfast was a silent, tense affair and over with quickly. Van Horn saddled his horse and rode off without a word. Milstead was going to call out to his brother, but Coppersmith stopped him. "Reckon he needs to be off on his own. Ain't the first time. He'll be back. Might even be in his right mind when he is."

"That'll be fine with me."

The two saddled their own horses, packed the mule, and rode out. They traveled without haste but without dawdling. They stopped at whatever farm or ranch they spotted and asked about the outlaws but did not get any helpful information.

Both men worried when Van Horn did not appear that night, nor the next day. Neither mentioned it, but both were aware of the other's concern.

Van Horn showed up midafternoon two days later. "We'll likely find 'em in Quarryville, down in the Nations," he said without preliminary.

"Can we make it today?" Milstead asked.

Van Horn nodded. "But it'd be around midnight. Ain't a good place to be in the dark, I hear. We stop soon, skip Arkansas City, and leave by daybreak we can be there late mornin', early afternoon."

"Know a place to camp or do we just plunk ourselves down here?"

"There's a stream with a few cottonwoods three, maybe four miles. It'll do well and won't take long to get there if we press on."

———

THEY RODE into Quarryville just before noon. As they clopped down what might've been called Main Street in a real town, the three kept wary eyes on the mostly tents housing saloons, a few restaurants and a couple of mercantiles. A dilapidated wooden building appeared to be a poor excuse for a bordello.

"Doesn't look like folks here are very amiable," Coppersmith said.

"Did you think they would be?" Van Horn growled.

Milstead and Coppersmith looked at each other and shrugged.

Suddenly Van Horn stopped. The other two, surprised, followed suit. They turned their horses at right angles to the street, so they could keep an eye on all the "establishments."

"Biddle! Bucky Biddle!" Van Horn yelled. "Get your pox-riddled hide out here, you mouse-humpin' scum. Time to pay for your many and heinous misdeeds."

Silence fell, and Van Horn let it stand for a few moments, then shouted, "Biddle, we know you're a lily-livered pus bucket, but have the stones to come out here and meet the man who's gonna put you in your grave."

"So you're the great Travis Van Horn, eh?" a voice came from behind them.

The three turned, and Van Horn moved a little out front of the others. He looked over the outlaw and the seven henchmen behind him. "So you're the great Bucky Biddle," Van Horn countered. "I thought you'd be a bigger fella, not some canker-covered pipsqueak."

Biddle looked as someone had just kicked him. "Big talk from a man about to die."

"I ain't the one about to die, you baby-stealin' shit pole."

"Ah, yes, the little girl. She wasn't really developed at all, but that didn't matter. She was a tasty little bit." His grin was oily.

Milstead glanced at his brother. Van Horn was already reaching for a Remington, his body stiff with rage.

"Don't, Travis," Milstead said urgently. "He's lyin'. He's just tryin' to rile you so you'll make mistakes. If he does, it might get us killed."

Van Horn fought to control his temper.

Into the breech, Coppersmith said, "Now, I know you ain't got the decency to not do that to a little girl, Biddle, but you don't have enough manhood to poke a flea, let alone a girl, even one that young."

"Travis," Milstead warned. When Van Horn turned eyes filled with rage toward his brother, Milstead added, "Jace is aimin' to rile Biddle into mistakes."

"And who are you?" Biddle asked, looking toward Coppersmith. "You're a mite young to be ridin' with these yahoos."

The bounty hunter smiled insolently. "I'm the fella who's gonna put three, maybe four of your chicken-humpin' pals into the ground, you pock-faced bucket of mule piss."

Almost spitting in rage, Biddle went for a pistol, as did his men.

"Now, Travis," Milstead said, drawing his own

revolver. Coppersmith had already let fly a couple of shots.

The three slid off their horses while bursts of gunfire roared from both sides.

———

IT WAS OVER IN LESS than a minute. Coppersmith had a bullet scrape across the outside of one thigh, Van Horn sported a bloody line across a cracked rib, Milstead was unharmed, but his horse was down, and he had to shoot it to put it out of its misery.

The three walked to where the eight outlaws lay. Four were dead. Biddle and three others were still alive but they were not long for this world.

Coppersmith, Milstead, and Van Horn each finished off one of Biddle's minions, then gathered around the outlaw leader where they reloaded all their revolvers.

"Your child-snatchin' days are over, Biddle," Van Horn said. He cocked his Remington and pointed it at Biddle's head. "Goodbye, scum."

"No, Travis!" Coppersmith shouted.

Van Horn looked at him, the fires of rage still blazing in his eyes.

"Killin' him that way is too good for him."

It took a few moments before Van Horn caught his friend's drift, and he nodded.

"You can shoot him in places that won't kill him, but they'll hurt real bad. Might take him a long time to die that way. Or you can stomp the snot out of him, break lots of bones."

"Or," Milstead, who had been watching for any possible retaliation from anyone, suggested over his shoulder, "you can do both."

"Now I have too many choices," Van Horn said, "Let me think a moment." He shot Biddle in his left kneecap. He looked almost as if it had been an accident. "Something must be wrong with this Remington to go off like that all on its own." He shot Biddle in the right thigh, breaking the femur but somehow missing the femoral artery. "There, it did it again. Is yours all right, Reese?"

Milstead took out a pistol and shot Biddle in the right forearm, shattering both the radius and ulna. "Looks like my Colt ain't workin' right either. Jace?"

Coppersmith shot the outlaw in the left upper arm, splintering the humerus. "Mine, too. Reckon we should head out right away and have 'em checked."

Milstead and Van Horn looked at each other for a moment, then each nodded. "Well, *adios*, Biddle," the latter said. "I suppose you won't mind if Reese here takes your horse, eh, since you shot his."

"Kill me, you bastard. Don't leave me here like this."

"Did you hear something, boys?" Van Horn asked.

"Just the wind."

The three walked off, ignoring Biddle's shouted pleas for release from his suffering.

As Milstead was saddling Rickett's horse with his own saddle, Coppersmith looked through the outlaw's saddlebags, surprised that they were there, though there were few safe places in the wretched town. He found some money.

"Look, Travis, Reese, a couple hundred dollars."

"What'd I tell you about rewards in this case?"

"And what did I tell you would happen if you said something like that to me again."

"Not now, boys," Milstead said.

"It ain't enough to figure out which bank it comes from and it probably came from more than one anyway.

But this here should provide the Muellers a bit of money to help with the new member of their family as well as for all the children."

"Sounds like a damn good idea," Milstead said. "Travis?"

"Reckon so," Van Horn grumbled.

They rode out of town and moved quickly, wanting to put as much distance between them and the outlaw town as they could. They finally stopped a couple hours after dark and made a swift, basic camp.

Coppersmith slept lightly and rose early. He quietly downed two cups of coffee, saddled his horse and rode off, heading north toward Kansas but not knowing where he would go.

A day of leisurely riding had him reaching the border between Kansas and the Indian Nations. He sat and looked around, wondering which way to go. Hundreds of miles to the northwest, Lily was lost to him. A bit to the west was Callie Seaver, a woman he had met only a few times but had come to admire. She was married, though, and very unlikely to return his affections. Behind him, somewhere in the Nations, was Missy Birch, the Pawnee whom he had fallen in love with, and she him before they were torn apart by her people's distrust of outsiders. She was sure to be married, too, by now, he figured.

There's Wichita, he thought as he made camp for the night even though there was still plenty of daylight left. Dan Quinn would certainly hire him as a deputy. Maybe continuing as deputy county sheriff was available. He laughed at that. He hadn't wanted the job when he was more or less forced to take it. He didn't even know where the badge was. He had liked his time as a lawman both in Wichita and in Blanca, but he was not sure he could say the same now.

He was no closer to a decision in the morning, so he saddled his bay gelding and rode north, crossing into Kansas early in the afternoon. He had figured while riding that Wichita was as good a place as any to go. Van Horn likely would stay away from the city, and Milstead would certainly go back to bounty hunting in the Nations.

There were also the German families, and they would accept him. Among those families were at least several girls of marriageable age. That was a bonus, Coppersmith thought. Maybe he could settle down. As a deputy marshal, he would make out all right financially what with a share of the taxes and fees the marshal collected. Being a deputy sheriff would pay reasonably well, too. With a respectable job and a decent income, maybe he could turn away from bounty hunting and instead get married and start a family. It was, he thought, a warm, pleasant picture.

He spent the night in Arkansas City, having a couple of beers, a good meal, and a few hours in what passed for a classy bordello here.

As he was saddling his horse in the morning, he made his decision. When he pulled out of the livery stable, he did not go north as he had been. This time he turned his nose southeast. "Fort Smith here I come," he muttered. He had decided that while becoming a lawman in Wichita and maybe marrying one of the German girls was a pleasant thought, he was sure it would not work out. Not for him. No, a return to the life he had been living before he was in on the search for Biddle was in the cards for him.

15

Time became meaningless to Coppersmith. He would pick up a handful of wanted posters, get a jail wagon, tie his horse behind it and head into the Nations. Weeks or months later, he would arrive back in Fort Smith, deposit his catch of outlaws, some alive, some not, and then have himself a spree. When that had run its course, he went through it all over again.

Though he had several acquaintances, he had no friends, nor did he need or want any. Friends, he thought more than once, were more trouble than they were worth.

A year after he had left Van Horn and Milstead, he ran into the latter in some festering sinkhole sarcastically called Purity by its not-so-illustrious citizens. Both were chasing the same outlaw gang.

They were standoffish with each other at first until each realized that other than chasing the same outlaw gang now, there was little competition between them. Not with all the outlaws roaming the Nations. There was also the fact that neither still had no liking for Travis Van Horn.

"What say we join forces, Reese?" Coppersmith asked as they were making ready to ride out of Purity, following the trail of the outlaws, who had fled.

"I thought that was what we were doin'."

"True. But I meant regular. Be safer for both of us, and we could share the work of cartin' these bastards around."

"And split the reward money."

Coppersmith nodded sadly. "Also true. Sorry I asked. Thought it might be a good idea. Reckon I was wrong."

"I didn't say I object to it. I only mentioned it to make sure you realized it. Thought you might not like to share."

"Just easin' my workload will be worth it." He grinned. "Besides, with the two of us we can catch twice as many outlaws, so we'd have that much more to split."

"I like that thinkin'."

———————

THE TRAIL LED north and two days later they rode into Arkansas City, Kansas, one of the towns they skirted in their hunt for Biddle more than a year ago.

"Some supper and we spend the night here?" Milstead asked.

"Sounds good to me. I'm tired of your cookin'."

"Yours ain't no better."

"Well, I can't disagree with you on that."

Both laughed.

They arrived in the afternoon and pulled the wagon into the yard at the livery stable.

"I don't want that damn thing here," the livery owner snapped.

"What you want doesn't matter a pig's tail to us," Coppersmith said. "We'll be leavin' in the mornin', so don't you go frettin' over things."

They took their saddlebags and rifles with them and found a room at the Walnut Creek House on North Summit Street near Walnut Ave. At the suggestion of the hotel clerk, they headed for Alvin's restaurant. On the way, Milstead said, "Damn, I forgot my wallet." He grinned. "Much as I'd like to, I can't expect you to pay for everything. Now, if only you paid your fair share." He laughed.

Coppersmith did, too, and slapped his companion on the upper arm with is hat.

"You go on, Jace. I won't be more than a few minutes."

Coppersmith nodded and walked off. Following the clerk's directions for a shortcut, he entered a narrow alley between a hardware store and a meat market to get to the restaurant on North First Street. Just as he was entering the alley from Summit Street, someone plowed into him, knocking him back into the alley and against the wall of the hardware store.

"Damn," he muttered as he shoved the man away. "Watch where you're goin', pal."

The man spun and launched a fist at Coppersmith, who jerked his head to the side but not enough to avoid all of the punch. It landed a glancing blow on his chin, snapping his head back a little.

"Son of a bitch," Coppersmith muttered. He blocked the man's next roundhouse and retaliated with a powerful shot to the man's midsection. The man doubled over with a loud *whoof* and staggered back a step.

A bullet suddenly splintered wood next to Copper-smith's head and he ducked, pulling a pistol as he did. He peeked around the corner, then immediately jerked back as two other shots rang out, thudding into the wall.

Still doubled over, the man he had punched stumbled out of the alley and across the street.

"What the hell?" he muttered. He peeked around the corner again, then shoved off to the wall on the other side. It left him a bit more exposed, but it allowed him to send off a couple of rounds of his own. He didn't hit anyone, but he sent the four men—including the one he had punched—scurrying for the cover of barrels, boxes, and a water trough across the street.

He pulled back and turned, ready to head down the alley the other way toward First Street, but two men, guns drawn, had appeared at the opening there. "Well, damn," he muttered.

"What the hell's goin' on here?" he yelled at the men just newly appeared. "I don't have anything against you fellas, whoever you are, nor them others, whoever they are, neither."

The only response he got was a couple of rounds from one of the new men's pistols. He thanked his stars that the men seemed to be mighty poor shots, as the bullets thudded harmlessly into the wall of the hardware store.

"You, out in the street," he hollered, "what's your beef with me, boys? All I was doin' was headin' for some grub. Don't know you or the boys down the alley."

"Go to hell, you backshootin' bastard!" someone yelled. "Killed our cousin after sidin' with those damned Cawley brothers."

"The devil you say!" roared one of the men at the other end of the alley. "You Hayes boys sent that bastard to kill Pa Cawley."

These sons a bitches are loco, Coppersmith thought. He was sweating now, caught between two apparently feuding factions out to kill someone—anyone—they came across who they thought was a member of the other faction.

"Look, boys, I don't know who the hell you are or what your disagreement with each other is, but I don't know a one of you and I sure as hell ain't takin' sides. Now let me on through so's I can get me some supper and you can shoot at each other all you desire to."

He looked up the alley and saw the two men, and apparently a third who was behind the meat market, arguing quietly among themselves. He turned his attention around the corner of the building where he stood and could hear the other group chatting from their hiding places, though he could not hear the words. He took the time to reload his pistol, then pulled the other one. He had no chance he figured if both sides started shooting, but at least this way he would have one six-gun to return fire in each direction.

Both sides had quieted down, but Coppersmith knew they were there, just behind the corners of the buildings on one side and the barrels, boxes, and trough on the other. Sweating, he considered his options. They were poor at best. "Damn," he finally mumbled again. Standing here boxed in by two groups of lunatics was not going to get him anywhere. The only way to go, he figured, was down the alley to First Street. The men on Summit were hidden behind various large containers; the ones on First were poor shots and hiding just around the corner of the walls. To shoot at him, they had to expose themselves. He could, he hoped, slide up that way without making too much noise.

Coppersmith took a deep breath and started creeping

down the alleyway toward First Street, keeping as close to the one wall as possible. His head seemed on a swivel, as he swung it back and forth, trying to keep an eye on both sides. Suddenly he froze when he saw a body fall across the entrance to the alley on First Street, followed by another, then a third.

A carrot-topped young man stood in the alley entrance, the light behind him casting an eerie glow on him. "Well, don't stand there all day, pard. C'mon."

Coppersmith walked toward Reese Milstead. At the end of the alley, he stopped and saw three men sprawled out unconscious.

"I could've killed all three, and maybe I should have, but I sent someone for Marshal Cleghorn, and he'll lock 'em up. But we still got the Hayes boys to deal with. And I won't much care about shootin' a couple of them. They're pretty bad fellas. I got a heap of paper on 'em."

"These ones aren't outlaws?"

Milstead shrugged. "If they are, I haven't seen paper on 'em. I think they're just family foolish enough to tangle with the Hayes boys."

"You aimin' to go after 'em?"

"*We're* goin' after 'em. Unless you ain't the man I been thinkin' you are all this time."

"Count me in. There's four of 'em. One's hidin' behind the water trough in front of Burk's Mercantile. The others are behind barrels and boxes on the sidewalk out front of the store."

Milstead nodded. "Go north from here and turn onto Walnut up to Summit, then down that toward the alley here."

"What'll you be doin'?"

"Headin' the other way down First to Chestnut, then over to Summit and come up on 'em from the south.

Catch 'em in a crossfire should they choose not to give up. We'll give 'em a chance to do so, but if they ain't inclined, don't hesitate to shoot 'em. They don't deserve consideration."

"Seems like you know a lot about this place."

"It's close to the Nations, so I've been through here more than a few times. Know the marshal pretty well, which is why I ain't worried about these other fellas here." He chucked his chin toward men lying at his feet. "Cleghorn's a good man but he's no man hunter, so he'll be mighty pleased if we rid the city of the Hayes boys."

Coppersmith nodded. "See you on the other side." He grinned.

"I might object to that if it means what it usually means," Milstead said, also with a grin. "Let's go."

A few minutes later, each turned the corner onto Summit Street and slowly moved toward the outlaws. When they were ten yards away on either side of the men, Coppersmith said, "You boys need to drop your weapons. You're under arrest."

Four heads turned to look at the young bounty hunter. One of them grinned. "You ain't good enough to take all of us, punk."

The others laughed, as all of them rose to their feet.

"Maybe not, but the two of us are," Milstead said.

Four heads cranked around so fast that Coppersmith though they might fall off.

"Now, do as I said, boys," Coppersmith warned.

"You two ain't gonna do nothin'," one of the men said with a chuckle.

Milstead shot him in the chest. The man fell, dead.

"Any of you others think we'll do nothin'?" When he got no response, he said, "Didn't think so. Now, do as my partner said and you might come out of this alive."

16

"Like hell," Clint Hayes snapped and yanked out a pistol. His two brothers did the same.

Fifteen seconds later, all three had joined their brother dead on the ground.

"I shouldn't be after all these years chasin' outlaws, but I'm still amazed at the stupidity of some of these fellas," Milstead said with a shake of the head.

"Well, I reckon I can understand it some, Coppersmith said. "They know that if they get taken in, they'll likely be hanged. And, bein' dumb as bricks, most of 'em, they think they can take anyone, especially if the good guys—that's us—are outnumbered."

"Reckon so, but you'd think at least some of 'em would learn from the fatal mistakes of others."

"They also got it in their heads that they're invincible."

Milstead shrugged. "Well, it ain't my job to worry about such things, just clean up the trash when necessary."

"How much are these fellas worth?"

"Three hundred for Clint, two hundred each on the others."

"Not a bad take, and we don't have to worry about the bodies."

"Nope, that's the city's job. Now let's go get something to eat. I'm hungry."

WITH FOUR HUNDRED fifty dollars each in his pocket, the two men set out to the northeast just after dawn the day after next. With wagon still empty, they headed for Dexter. In their day and a half in Arkansas City waiting for the reward money, they had heard that Clancy McDermott and his gang had robbed a bank in Dexter.

They were in no hurry—the robbers would not hang around the town—but they didn't dally either and pulled into Dexter not long after dark. They got a room at a cheap hotel on the outskirts of town and were asleep soon after supping. In the morning, they paid a visit to Marshal Claude Wellington, who was glad to see them.

"Lawmen sometimes ain't happy with our kind," Coppersmith said.

"Hell, if you can catch bastards like McDermott and the devils that ride with him, you'd get my vote in any election you wanted to run in. I'm a good lawman, but I ain't equipped to deal with men like [last name]."

"Not many town marshals are," Milstead said. "What happened exactly?"

"Ain't much to tell. Three of 'em went inside the bank and two others waited right outside. Bank teller apparently wasn't fast enough handing over the money, so one of the bastards shot him in the heart. Killed him." There was a sense of wonder in his voice that such a thing could happen. "That raised some alarm. One of 'em shot a customer in the bank. Killed him too. "Then those damn outlaws shot three more people as they galloped out of town. One of them died, too."

"Didn't anybody try to stop 'em durin' or after?" Coppersmith asked.

"By the time we got some people armed, those fellas were long gone. A posse went out after 'em, but there wasn't much heart in it. Except for a deputy, they were all townsmen, and they were not about to face down a gang of outlaws."

"Can't say as I blame 'em."

"Me neither, Mr. Coppersmith. If only we could—" He sighed and shook his head. "Well, wishes don't mean spit in a case like this."

"We'll see what we can do, Marshal," Milstead said. "Any idea of where they might go after committin' some of their deviltry?"

"If not in the Nations, I heard they have kin in and around Cedar Vale, maybe a day's ride, seventeen miles or so southeast of here."

"Obliged."

"You leavin' right away?"

"Reckon not," Coppersmith said. "The horses need rest after haulin' that jail wagon around for several weeks now."

"I can watch over it for you if you boys want to move lighter. You catch those boys alive, you can bring 'em back here to transport 'em to Fort Smith in that wagon. If they ain't alive, well you won't need that wagon for 'em."

"Can we trust you?" Coppersmith asked, a slight grin on his lips.

"Have I ever lied to you boys?"

Milstead laughed. "Unless you've done so in the few minutes we've been talkin', I can't say as you have." The laughter dropped. "Of course, if you *are* lyin' about what happened or are sendin' us into a trap, me and Jace here will be mighty displeased."

Wellington gulped but did not drop his gaze. "I ain't lyin'. God's truth."

The two bounty hunters looked at each other and nodded. "Then you got a deal, Marshal," Coppersmith said. "We left the wagon at the stables last night, but we only asked for the horses to be cared for regular. Figured today we'd take better care of 'em, even if just to give 'em a rest. With this new arrangement, we expect the animals to get special care. Just make sure he does a good job."

"I will. Clem's a good man."

"We'll have us some grub, then pick up a few supplies —just enough for a couple three days—saddle up and head out. Should be gone in about an hour."

The marshal nodded. "I figure I know what you'll need. I'll stop by Caldwell's and get the stuff ready for you." He shrugged apologetically. "You'll have to pay for 'em, of course. The city might look prosperous but it ain't rich enough to provide even that, though I sure would if I could."

"We don't mind payin' our way."

Wellington nodded. "Just stop by Caldwell's when you're ready. He'll have everything ready."

Since it was late in the day, they didn't make too much progress before they made camp, then got back on the road in the morning.

———

A FEW HOURS BEFORE DARK, they spotted a rider coming from the barn on a farm a couple of miles outside Cedar Vale. They became aware of movement around the house and few outbuildings and near the cottonwoods and willows lining Cedar Creek.

"This don't look so good, Jace," Milstead said.

"Nope. Ain't much we can do about it but keep ridin' and hopin' we can talk our way out of any trouble that arises, or shoot out way out if not, and it sure as hell seems like trouble is comin'."

The two stopped when the rider did, about ten yards apart. "What're you boys doin' here abouts?" the rider asked.

"Just passin' through."

"Headin' where?"

"East," Coppersmith said flatly.

"I didn't ask what direction, I asked where was you goin'."

"Can't see that it's any of your business, friend."

"I ain't your friend and I'd be obliged if you was to tell me where you're goin'."

"Like I said, it's none of your concern. We're just passin' through, maybe stop for some grub, then mosey on."

"You ain't moseyin' nowhere 'less'n you tell me where you're headin'."

"Just get the hell out of the way, mister," Coppersmith snapped. "Either move or we'll ride over you."

"The devil you will." The man began levelling his rifle at them.

Coppersmith and Milstead yanked out pistols and fired at the same time. Two bullets punched holes in the rider's chest.

But it set off a fusillade from all around.

Coppersmith's horse went down, and he grunted as a bullet pierced his side, just under the armpit, and exited at an angle out the back. He managed to jump clear of the mount as it went down, and he took what protection he could from the jerking animal. He finally had to shoot it in the head so it would stop kicking and trying to rise, which had made it damn difficult to use it for something of a fortification. He reached out and grabbed his Winchester and began firing slowly but steadily.

Milstead snatched his Winchester out of the scabbard and slid out of the saddle. He tried controlling his horse to no avail, so he let the animal go. A moment after the horse bolted, leaving him wide open, the bounty hunter took a bullet just under the lowest left rib. As he was falling, another slug caught him high on the right side of the chest and spurted out the back. "Damn," he muttered as he fell.

"Reese? You all right, Reese?"

"Just dandy," he gasped. "You pay attention to yourself and keep on firin' at those boys over by the buildings."

"Ah, hell, and here I was gonna take a rest while you took care of things. Now I got to work because you let yourself get shot." He fired a few more rounds and heard at least one man howl as if he had been hit.

"Let myself get shot?" Milstead gasped in return, making it as lighthearted as he could with his wounds.

"Well, maybe not *let* yourself. You gonna be all right?"

"Ain't sure but now ain't the time to worry about it."

Things quieted down for a bit, and Coppersmith said, "Best reload, if you're able. I got a feelin' they're gonna rush us soon. I think they think we're both down."

"Let 'em come," Milstead said, but his voice wavered and had a note of pain in it.

"Hold on, Reese. Soon's we get out of this, I'll get you to a doctor back in Dexter."

"Might not be necessary."

"I know. But those bastards'll pay dearly for puttin' us under."

"Amen to that, Jace." He coughed, then groaned a little. "Dammit all," he muttered.

Suddenly three men burst forth from inside the barn, and four darted out from the trees, all letting fly a steady barrage of lead as they raced forward.

Coppersmith and Milstead provided their own volley. Milstead, lying out in the open, had a bullet take off a piece of his ear and another scrape across his scapula as he lay there. But he kept firing and before the three men who were charging him had gotten halfway to him, the bounty hunter had laid waste to them.

A dozen or so bullets plowed into the horse Coppersmith was sheltering behind, and he flinched each time a hunk of lead hit, but he remained calm and fired carefully, steadily. Three went down quickly. The fourth made it to within five feet of the bounty hunter before Coppersmith put a slug into him. The man stumbled forward a bit and fell across the dead horse.

"How's things on your side, Reese?"

"Got 'em all."

"They dead?"

"Ain't sure. But I reckon so. None of 'em is movin'. Your side?"

"I got 'em all, too. I think one of 'em is tryin' to crawl back to the trees. I'll make sure of him, then check your side. Just stay where you are. Conserve your strength."

Milstead just grunted in response.

Coppersmith checked all the outlaws on his side and had to finish one off with a bullet to the head. Then he checked the ones Milstead had shot, and he finally, carefully, checked the house and the barn. All were empty.

He reloaded the Winchester and tossed it into the bed of a small farm wagon, then began hurriedly hitching up a team to it. He drove it out, stopping next to Milstead. "Come on, Reese, time to get you some help."

"You're not gonna take all these boys with us? Reckon there's rewards on most of 'em if not all of 'em."

"You can't ride up front with me."

"I can rest on the pile of bodies."

"You sure?"

"Yep." He laughed, though it was forced and set off a spasm of coughing. "What the hell, I might be joinin' 'em soon. It'd save you the trouble of haulin' me up there."

"You ain't joinin' 'em if I can help it." Coppersmith went around and tossed each body into the wagon bed. He finally stopped next to Milstead again. "All right, partner, up you go. Don't know how much of a cushion these boys'll provide but it might be better than the wood," he said as he helped his companion into the wagon.

17

Milstead was still conscious but barely when the wagon driven by Coppersmith rode into Dexter and pulled to a stop in front of Dr. Pete Clifford's office. Despite his wanting to get Milstead to the doctor, Coppersmith had kept his speed down so as not to jostle his partner too much on the bumpy ride, so it was after dawn when they arrived.

Hearing the noise, Clifford stepped outside. "I hope they all aren't sick," he said somewhat jovially. It was easy for him—or anyone else—to tell that all the men in the wagon but one were no longer among the living.

Coppersmith jumped off the wagon seat and helped Milstead down from the back.

"He doesn't look so good," Clifford said dryly.

"You're gonna look like him, or maybe the others, you keep up that line of talkin'," Coppersmith snapped, worry deep in his voice.

"Pshaw. Come, get him into my office quickly. I might make jokes, but I do care about my patients."

Coppersmith helped Milstead onto the examining

table, and Clifford cut off his shirt. "Didn't you do anything for him?" the doctor asked Coppersmith.

"Drove all night to get him to you to get fixed up."

Clifford looked as if he were going to say something but then just nodded. He began examining his patient, then said over his shoulder, "You may go now, Mr....?"

"Jace Coppersmith."

"You may go, Mr. Coppersmith. I work better without an audience, especially one who appears to be cantankerous."

"Oh, I'm irritable all right. I—" He stopped when Marshal Claude Wellington walked in. "And the reason for me being ornery just arrived."

"You talkin' about me?" Wellington asked, surprised.

"Yes, you, boy. I told you what would happen if you sent me and Reese into a trap. That's just what you did." He began to unlimber a Colt.

"Take it outside, Mr. Coppersmith," Clifford said. "I'll not have gunplay in my office. And I'd be obliged if you would refrain from shooting the marshal, or anyone else, for a spell. One gunshot patient at a time is enough."

"Outside, Marshal," Coppersmith ordered.

Pasty white with fear, Wellington turned and walked out followed by Coppersmith. The lawman was acutely aware of the gun pointed at his spine. "Listen, I didn't send you and your friend into a trap," the lawman said as they stopped beside the wagon.

"I ain't in a mood to listen to your lies, Marshal. Now get up in the back of that wagon so that when I shoot you dead, I don't have to pick you up and toss you up there with your friends."

"I don't know a single one of those fellows, though I saw Clancy and Liam when they robbed the bank. That's as close to any of the McDermotts I got."

"I don't believe you."

"You gotta. I'm tellin' you the truth."

Coppersmith looked around. A small but growing crowd had begun to gather, and the bounty hunter decided shooting Wellington in the back in front of all these people would not be a good idea. He holstered his Colt and plucked out Wellington's revolver, which he kept pointed at the marshal. "Up on the seat, Marshal, and drive. We'll take us a little ride down to the boneyard and drop these fellas off. Save me some work, too, when I send you to join your friends there."

"I told you, they ain't my friends."

"And I told you I don't believe you. How else would those boys know who we were and be lyin' in wait for us if you didn't warn 'em?"

"I don't know, dammit. I just know it wasn't me."

"Who else could've done it?"

"I ain't sure. Like I said, McDermott has kin over in Cedar Vale. He might here, too. Maybe one of his kinfolks was in town, heard about you headin' out that way and rode out to warn 'em."

"And I don't suppose you'd know who that was either."

"I don't. Like I said, I don't know—didn't know—McDermott or any of his men. Didn't know any of his family either, really, except maybe one cousin, and I didn't see him in town." He paused. "And how would I have gotten there before you? You boys left before I did."

Coppersmith was beginning to think that Marshal Wellington was telling the truth, but he was not certain at all, and that made him uncomfortable. If Wellington wasn't lying, the bounty hunter would have to go after whoever it was who might've betrayed them. But that meant finding out who it was, and he had no idea how to do that in an unfamiliar town. If the lawman was lying, Coppersmith might not have a way of proving it and thus would be in danger. Being wounded, Milstead would be in even more danger.

Wellington pulled the wagon to a stop at the edge of the cemetery. Arthur Brock, who had been following the slow-moving wagon on foot stopped alongside the marshal. "Looks like you got a load of bodies there, Claude," said Brock, whose fiefdom was the cemetery and its associated functions.

"Not my doin', Art. Mr. Coppersmith is responsible. He and a friend. And rightly so. They were bushwhacked by McDermott and his kin."

"Nasty bunch, those boys. The world's a better place without 'em." He looked over at Coppersmith. "What's your plan for these fellows?"

"That's your concern, not mine."

"Who'll pay for it?"

"That's not my concern either."

When Brock looked at Wellington, the marshal said hastily, "The city doesn't have the money, Art."

"Go through their pockets," Coppersmith said. "Use whatever you find to pay for it. If it ain't enough, just pile 'em up, toss some kerosene on 'em and set a match to the pile. You can burn the wagon, too, if it'll help. Just bring the horses down to the livery when you're done."

Coppersmith and Wellington hopped down off the wagon. The bounty hunter pulled the cartridges out of the marshal's pistol and handed it back to him.

"Ya know, Mr. Coppersmith, if you left my pistol loaded and shot me, you could claim self-defense."

"Reckon I could." He shrugged. "Reckon I ain't quite ready to put you in the boneyard there with your friends."

I told you they—"

"I know."

As they walked toward town, the lawman said, "You better have your own wound looked after."

"It'll be all right."

"You don't get it tended it could start to fester, and that wouldn't be good at all."

"Worried about me now?"

"Look, Mr. Coppersmith," Wellington said nervously, "I know you think I'm a liar and all, but I ain't, and I think I'm a decent fella, one who cares what happens to others."

"Even if that fella doesn't like you?"

"Yes." His voice had firmed up.

Coppersmith looked at him in surprise. "Reckon I will have it tended once the doc is done fixin' Reese. You'll be right beside me, though."

"Figured as much."

Clifford was still working on Milstead, but he glanced at Coppersmith and Wellington when they arrived and took chairs. "I'm almost disappointed," the physician said. "Like I figured, only one more patient for me. I thought the other would be up with Arthur now."

"Might still be," Wellington said, voice once again worried.

Clifford was done soon and turned to Coppersmith. "Well, let's take a look at you."

"What about Reese?" he nodded his head toward his friend.

"I gave him something to put him to sleep for a bit. He'll be all right, I reckon. He's a strong young man, the bullets went clear through and, better, they didn't hit anything vital. Looks like the same goes for you."

Clifford soon had Coppersmith's wounded cleaned,

lightly coated with Lugol's solution, and bandaged. "You'll be fine in a week or so, Mr. Coppersmith. Just don't go doing anything too strenuous."

The bounty hunter nodded.

"So what happens to me?" Wellington asked. His tone was one of resignation, though he still held out some hope. He thought that because Coppersmith hadn't killed him yet that the bounty hunter might never do so.

"I'll think about it. For now, we go to your office where we'll chat a bit."

———

"YOU HAVE no idea who could've done this if you didn't, Marshal?" Coppersmith asked. He had a cup of coffee laced with an ounce of rotgut to fortify himself. He felt a little weak from the loss of blood and thought the libation might keep him going. He was afraid that if he fell asleep, Wellington would kill him if indeed the lawman was lying.

"No. Like I told you, I don't know any of them except a passing acquaintance with one who might be a cousin. Or might not. I don't know him well enough to be certain."

———

"MR. COPPERSMITH, WAKE UP. MR. COPPERSMITH."

The bounty hunter groggily opened his eyes, hand instinctively reaching for a Colt. But he stopped when he saw Wellington. It took him a moment to realize he was not dead, that the lawman had not killed him. "Reckon I nodded off," he mumbled.

"That you did."

"How long?"

"Couple hours."

"And you didn't shoot me?"

"Does it feel like I did?"

"Why? Or, rather, why not?"

"I'm not a killer, Mr. Coppersmith, though I've been called to do so on one occasion. Most of my duties are mundane, arresting drunks, breaking up a brawl now and again, collecting taxes and fees. Rarely any gunplay."

"But I was gonna—"

"No you weren't. I concluded that an hour or so ago. If you were gonna, you would've done so already. For a while there I thought you were a killer." He held up his hand to cut off any comment from Coppersmith. "Oh, you've killed men, lots of 'em I'm sure, but I don't think you're a cold-blooded killer, a man who shoots people down for the hell of it. Once I realized that, I figured I could try to find out who helped set up that trap."

"And did you?"

"I think so, yes."

"Who?"

"Fella name Donnell Sullivan. Clem over at the livery says he thinks Sullivan's been courtin' one of the McDermott girls. He said Sullivan left here a little while before you did, ridin' as if the devil himself was nibblin' at his ass."

"You believe it?"

"Yes."

"And I should believe you?"

"Yes." Wellington sighed but when he spoke, exasperation was in his voice. "Look, Mr. Coppersmith, if I wanted to harm you, even kill you, I had plenty of opportunity. You were asleep. It would've been easy to put a slug or two into your head. But I didn't. I didn't even whack you over the head to knock you out and toss you in a cell 'til you wised up."

Coppersmith thought about it a few moments, then nodded. "You're right, Marshal. I'm thankful you didn't kill me, and I'm obliged that you found out who laid a trap for us. If he really is the man."

"Don't you believe me, dammit?"

"I do. But we don't know for sure if he was the one. We can only presume he was the one."

"So, what do we do?"

"Don't know yet. Something to eat might get my head movin' again so I can think."

As they were finishing up their lunch, a townsman walked in, spotted Wellington, and walked over. "What can I do for you, Cal?"

The man glanced at Coppersmith but nodded when the marshal said it was all right to talk in front of the bounty hunter.

"I stayed the night in Cedar Vale last night and heard people sayin' a couple of bounty men gunned down a bunch of the McDermott and Sullivan men. Just shot 'em in cold blood."

"That's horse shit," Coppersmith snapped.

Cal's eyes widened when he glanced at the bounty hunter. "Anyway, I heard 'em say they were gonna send the rest of the McDermott men here to take care of business."

"Had they left before you did?" Coppersmith asked.

"I didn't see 'em on the road, so I reckon not. I rode hard as I could to get here as fast as I could to warn you, Marshal."

"Thanks, Cal." When the man left, Wellington asked, "So *now* what do we do?"

"Face 'em and put an end to it. Have somebody up in the church tower keepin' an eye on the road. When they spot the McDermott boys, tell him to ring the bell. I'll take it from there."

"But you—"

"This is my line of business, Marshal, not yours. Oh, and pass the word around now that when the bell rings, folks should get inside and stay there. Now finish your lunch and take care of your part of the business."

18

COPPERSMITH WAS SURPRISED THAT THE TOWN of Dexter basically became a ghost town when the church bell rang. He had known many a place where residents would not have listened to what the marshal said in such a circumstance. Either the people of Dexter were smarter than their counterparts elsewhere or Marshal Wellington was quite persuasive.

The bounty hunter came out of the hotel and checked his weapons as he leaned against the wall under the portico. Then he waited.

It was only minutes before five men rode into town and stopped, looking confused. There was no activity in town, no mounted men riding around, no wagons being loaded, no people walking around, no children playing, no loud clanging from the blacksmith shop. It was eerie even to Coppersmith.

"Where is everybody?" one of the men called. He shrugged when he got no answer, and he and his fellows started up again. Coppersmith strode out into the street and stopped when the men were maybe fifteen yards away. They stopped when a little closer.

"I suggest you boys turn yourselves around and ride back to wherever you came from. Cedar Vale'd be my guess."

"And why should we do that?" the same man asked with a sneer.

"Because I asked you nicely."

"Who the hell are you?"

"Doesn't really matter. I'm just the man warnin' you to leave Dexter."

"If we don't?" The man seemed to be quite jolly.

"Then you'll die."

The man laughed. "You think you can take the five of us?"

"Don't know. I aim to find out, though, if you boys don't ride on out of here." A hand moved up stealthily to rest on the butt of one Colt.

Coppersmith dropped to one knee as he drew his revolver and fired. He hit the leader once in the chest and once in the stomach, then swung toward the man on the leader's right. The man's horse was prancing. Making aiming impossible, but the bounty bunter fired anyway, one bullet plowing into the man's right side and exploding out the left.

A bullet clipped Coppersmith in the shoulder near the neck. The shock of it knocked his aim off, and his next two shots went wide. He holstered that Colt and grabbed the other. Before he could fire, one of the three men left went down. A moment later Coppersmith heard the crack of a rifle.

The bounty hunter fired twice again, hitting one of the men in the head and in the throat, both lucky shots considering that man's horse was also bouncing around.

The last of the men turned and raced away, but he too went down, followed an instant later by another rifle crack.

Coppersmith rose and turned, looking up the street. Marshal Wellington came out from behind a building holding a Winchester, barrel resting on his shoulder, lever pointing to the sky.

"You?" the bounty hunter asked in disbelief.

"Yep." Wellington looked proud but pasty.

"You're looking a bit peaked, Marshal. Maybe you better sit a spell."

"I'll be all right."

"That was some shootin'. But why'd you do it?"

"Dexter's my town, and I'm charged with protectin' the citizens of it."

"I ain't a citizen."

"Well, true, but if you got killed, those boys might've hurt some of the folk here, and I couldn't abide that. Plus, you're a visitor to Dexter, which makes you a temporary citizen in my eyes."

"I've never been thought of a citizen of any town before," he lied, "so I'm obliged," He paused. "Seems like there's more. Something you haven't told me."

"Yes. I couldn't bear the thought of you thinkin' I'd sent you and your friend into a trap when it wasn't true. I felt it my duty to help remove some of the scum who caused all the trouble and nearly killed your friend."

"Thanks, Marshal. It takes a lot for most people to shoot someone down like you did."

"You don't seem to have any trouble."

"Well, that's a fact. I've done so a lot, way too much I sometimes think. I try to avoid it, but it seems I don't succeed in that very often."

"Why'd you go out and face 'em like that? Seems

foolish when you could've stood behind a building like I did and just blasted away at 'em."

"A few reasons," Coppersmith said with a crooked smile, "the main one being stupidity. There's also a certain amount of bravado. A man in my profession gets cocky sometimes, a feelin' that could be fatal. But there's something comes up inside us sometimes where we want to face down a group because we think we can't be killed, or even hurt."

"Doesn't work, I reckon." Wellington pointed to Coppersmith's shoulder.

"That's also true. Fortunately, I don't get that stupid too often. And I've been lucky that outlaws haven't been better shots, though some have been mighty good."

"Been shot worse?"

"Yep."

"Now it's my turn to say I sense there's even more."

Coppersmith sighed. "Sometimes bein' foolish is to think I can make something happen, though it ain't at all likely, and I know it."

"I don't understand."

"I was hopin' those boys'd turn and ride out of here without causin' trouble. Didn't really figure they would, but I had to try. There's been enough killin' lately."

"I'm surprised to hear you say that," Wellington said.

Coppersmith glared at the lawman and walked away, bumping the marshal's shoulder as he went."

"Jace, wait," Wellington shouted, but Coppersmith did not stop.

The bounty hunter went straight to Dr. Clifford's. The physician took one look at him and grinned. "I hope you and your friend plan to stay in Dexter for a while."

"Doubt it. Why?"

"With all the business you bring, I'll get rich." He laughed.

"Glad we can be of service. Now, if you'd be so kind as to stop your not so funny comedy show, I'd be obliged if you'd see to my wound."

"Of course, of course. Come, sit in this chair." As he worked, the doctor said, "That was some show you put on, Mr. Coppersmith."

"Maybe, but I'd be over at Brock's instead of here if it wasn't for Marshal Wellington."

"I thought I saw a couple of those outlaws go down without you firing at them and figured someone with a rifle was firing from behind you. That was the marshal?"

"Yes. I didn't know he was plannin' it but I'm sure glad he was there."

"I can imagine. Where is the marshal now? I'd think he'd be here with you."

"I'm afraid I drove him off. When I told him there had been enough killin' for today, he said he was surprised to hear that from a bounty hunter."

"Many people feel that way." He stepped back. "All done."

"I know, but I thought Wellington was a better man than that."

"He is. But he's not used to killing, and he's not used to bounty hunters. Fellows like you have a reputation of shooting instead of trying to arrest outlaws."

"I ain't like that."

"Perhaps not, but Marshal Wellington only knows what he has heard and what he has seen. You bringing in a wagonload of dead outlaws could only make him think you and Mr. Milstead are bloodthirsty bounty hunters."

"Reckon you're right," Coppersmith said after a few moments thought. "Speakin' of Reese, how's he doin'?"

"He'll be fine. I'm making sure he rests. That's the best thing for him now that I've patched him up. It'd be good for you, too."

"I'll see about gettin' some." He rose. "Well, thanks, Doc. Oh, and it may not make you rich," he said with a smile, "but I reckon me and Reese owe you for your doctorin'."

"I was wondering when you'd remember that I don't serve patients for free. Ten dollars ought to cover it."

Coppersmith handed him a gold double eagle. "A little extra in case it's needed."

"Thank you, Jace is it?"

Coppersmith nodded and walked out. Despite feeling the pain and having a desire to sleep, he headed for Wellington's office. He found the marshal sitting at his desk with an empty glass in his hand and an open bottle on the desk. "Gettin' drunk won't help, Marshal."

"I know. I only had one. I was considerin' another one, or maybe the whole bottle."

Coppersmith sat. "Like I said earlier, I appreciate what you did for me. What I didn't say was I'm sorry I treated you poorly. I reckon any dealin's you might've had with bounty hunters, or even any stories of 'em, made you think all of us are bloodthirsty savages. We ain't."

Wellington stared at him a minute, then nodded and placed the glass on the table. "So what happens now?"

"What do you mean?"

"I imagine all those men have prices on their head and I imagine you want that reward money. How do you get it?"

"From here, the best I can think of is to wire the U.S. marshal in Topeka and tell him those boys are dead. You should name 'em if you can, describe 'em if you don't know. If the marshal's competent, he'll wire back with a voucher or some such that will make your bank hand over the money."

"I'll do it right away. Go get yourself some rest." As Coppersmith turned to leave, Wellington said, "And, thank you, Mr. Coppersmith, you and Mr. Milstead, for removin' those reprehensible men from our area."

Coppersmith nodded and left.

————

THE NEXT DAY, Wellington met Coppersmith for lunch at Mackey's restaurant. "Marshal Abernathy up in Topeka acted fast. I got a wire here that says we—you— get the money. Twenty-four hundred dollars." There was awe in his voice. Wellington had never seen that much money at one time.

"Two hundred apiece. Not bad. We'll wander over to the bank and get the cash soon as we finish here."

Wellington nodded sadly.

Half an hour later, gold and silver coins in hand, Coppersmith and Wellington went to the marshal's office. The bounty hunter opened the two sacks and pulled out the coins. In minutes he had two piles.

"Splittin' with Mr. Milstead?" the lawman asked.

"Yep, it's the way we work."

"But he wasn't with you yesterday."

"Doesn't matter. We split whatever reward money we get. If he had been out there yesterday and I was layin' in Doc Clifford's office Reese'd be countin' this into two equal piles right now."

Wellington shook his head. "You are the strangest bounty hunter I've ever heard of." Seeing some anger cross Coppersmith's face he added, "I said *heard*. I never knew a bounty hunter before. You ain't what I expected."

Coppersmith nodded and smiled. He did some more counting and handed Wellington some coins. "Six hundred."

"What's this for?" the marshal stammered.

"The reward for your part in yesterday's fracas. You killed two of those boys."

"But at two hundred each, that's only four hundred. You just handed me six hundred."

"Call it a bonus for backin' me up."

"But that leaves you with only six hundred dollars while Mr. Milstead gets twelve hundred."

"Like I said, we split the reward money evenly. We don't necessarily split the expenses evenly. Now go deposit that in the bank but keep a little out and treat the missus to something special."

Coppersmith went to Dr. Clifford's. Milstead was awake and annoyed because the physician would not let him leave yet. "Been a pain in the ass, has he, Doc?" Coppersmith asked with a laugh. When Clifford nodded, he added, "See what I have to put up with all the time. It's tryin' on a man."

"Bah," Milstead snapped. He saw the sacks. "Reward money?"

"Yep. Two hundred each, includin' the ones yesterday."

"Doc told me about that."

Wellington moseyed in. "Thought I'd come see how you were doin', Mr. Milstead. Did Mr. Coppersmith tell you he gave me six hundred—" He clamped his mouth shut when Coppersmith glared at him.

Looking a bit confused, Milstead opened the sack that

his partner had handed him and counted. There's twelve hundred here."

"Yep. We got seven of those boys out in Cedar Vale and five here yesterday. The marshal shot two of em, so I gave him four hundred plus two hundred as a bonus."

"And you took it all out of your share?"

"Yep." Coppersmith glared at Wellington again.

"Damn fool," Milstead snapped. "We're partners, everything is half for you, half for me."

"That's what you got, half the twenty-four hundred."

"Well, the marshal's share should've come out of our share, not just yours." He counted some coins and held them out. When Coppersmith hesitated, Milstead said, "Take it dammit or I'll have to get up and kick your ass."

Coppersmith took the money and laughed. "Even on your best day you couldn't kick my ass."

"We'll see," Milstead growled, then he joined the others in laughing.

19

"YOU EVER THINK OF GETTIN' OUT OF THIS business, Reese, and maybe settlin' down?" Coppersmith asked one day as he and Milstead sipped beers in one of the many saloons in Dexter. It was two weeks after the battle with McDermott's gang of outlaws, and both men were still recovering.

"Yep. Even actually tried it once."

"Really?" Coppersmith was surprised.

Milstead nodded. "Me and Travis had helped a woman and her son get away from some outlaws down in the Nations."

"How did a woman and son—I presume they were good people—get caught by outlaws in the Nations?"

"She said they were headed to Texas when her husband took a wrong turn somewhere and they wound up deep in the Territory not knowing where they were. Some outlaws found 'em and killed the husband. The men brought her to a town down there, plannin' to have their way with her and let other members of the gang who were there have a go at her, too." Rage had crept into his voice.

"I wanted to ignore it, but Travis bein' the do-gooder that he is—well, was, no telling what he is these days—jumped into the middle of things, so I had to join him. We took Kate and Davey, who was nine at the time, across the Red River and into Texas and found some trustworthy fellas to get her to a town called McKinney. Then he and I went back to the Nations to finish our business there. When we had, I decided to go to McKinney and see if Kate would let me court her. I hadn't been very friendly to her on the trail but despite that she seemed to sense that I favored her. So off I went."

"So, it didn't work out," Coppersmith said, stating the obvious.

"Nope. I courted her a bit, then moved into her place outside of town a little way. Tried farmin' and a little ranching. I never was any good at farmin', even as a kid. It was one of the reasons Travis and I didn't get along. And I found I didn't have the patience or ability to make ranching a profitable concern, even a mild one. Me and Kate began to fight all the time. Well, not fight, just argue, 'til we both realized it wasn't workin' and we startin' thinkin' it might be time for me to move on. Travis showin' up and askin' me to help him run down a fella who'd killed someone up near Wichita and who he tracked to Texas. It gave me an excuse to leave. I still had some bounty money left, so I made sure she would be taken care of until she could get on her feet and rode off. I miss her. She was a good woman. I miss Davey, too. Never thought I could like a child, at least not one who wasn't my own, but I had come to see Davey as a son."

"I know the feelin'." Coppersmith's thoughts drifted

back to Texas, too, and a boy named Clay Dawes who Coppersmith had found after the boy's parents had been murdered by an outlaw gang. The bounty hunter had spent several days with the boy before taking him to a town and making sure he had good home with loving new parents. He found it strange at the time how hard it was leaving the boy. But he still thought of Clay now and again with a sense of loss.

Milstead looked at him in surprise, and Coppersmith explained Clay's story.

"Looks like we're both a little more soft-hearted than we like to think when it comes to children."

"Reckon so, especially five-year-old girls who may or not be related to two of those tough ol' bounty hunters."

Milstead smiled and raised his glass. They clinked them in a toast to soft-hearted hard men.

"So, you thinkin' of givin' settled life a try, Jace?"

"I ain't sure."

"With that gal over in Colorado Territory?"

"Lily? Hell. I expect she's already married to someone. It's been well over a year, gettin' near to two since I left Blanca. But maybe there's someone else out there for me who it'll be worth puttin' away my guns for."

"I hope you find her, Jace, but speakin' from experience, it ain't gonna happen."

"Worked for Travis, at least for a while."

"Yep, 'til some damn fool called on him to put on his guns again and ride off to help a friend, well, brother. Something neither of us'd do if we were married." He smiled sadly.

They were silent for a bit until Coppersmith asked, "How're you feelin', Reese?"

"Could be better, could be worse. Hell, I *have* been worse. Why do you ask? Thinkin' of leavin' soon?"

"Had crossed my mind."

"I can be ready whenever you are." Seeing Copper-smith's contemplative look, Milstead asked, "You thinkin' of not headin' to the Nations?"

"Might be foolish. But yeah, that's what I'm thinkin'."

"Gonna go searchin' for that imaginary gal who's gonna take you into her heart and turn you into a happy go lucky farm boy?" He grinned.

"Something like that."

"Damn fool, but it ain't my way to say nay to a man who's got his mind made up, even if it is on some crazy idea."

"Might be. But I reckon I got to try. It almost worked with Lily."

"Yep, almost."

Coppersmith grimaced. "And I don't have to be a farm boy. I can go back to bein' a lawman."

"I suppose you can," Milstead said thoughtfully. "Where? Wichita?"

"It was my thought, yeah."

"What about Travis?"

"What about him?"

"Way he was last time we saw him won't do well for a happy reunion."

"I ain't worried." Coppersmith shrugged. "I don't expect he's there, or at least not enough for it to be a problem. He might be hangin' on the fringes tryin' to keep an eye on Lizette from afar, but I doubt he's livin' in the city. If he is, I'll deal with it."

"Why take the risk?"

"Don't know anywhere else to go, really. I'm sure Dan will hire me back as a deputy." He grinned. "Might even see if I can still be a county sheriff's deputy. If I can find the damn badge."

Both laughed.

"If I were to guess, I'd say there was another reason for Wichita in particular."

Coppersmith grinned again. "Well, there are the two Vogel girls."

"Who are they?"

"Marina's tall and slender, a willowy beauty. Her sister, Ursula, is shorter and a bit on the plump side, though in a pleasin' way. I don't know which I'd prefer. Marina's a tad standoffish, with an air like she thinks she's better than other folk. Ursula, on the other hand, well, she's playful, quick to laugh."

"Seems like you took pretty good notice of those two gals in the brief times you were up that way."

"I always notice fine-lookin' women. Just because you're a blind old man without a likin' for young women don't mean every man is."

Milstead laughed. "Well, since I'm an old man, I'd have been lookin' over their mama. if I was there. Too bad she's married, though, I reckon."

Both laughed again.

"Good chance that if those Vogel gals are lookers like you say, they'll be married now."

"Could be. Marina'd be about seventeen or eighteen now, Ursala maybe a year or so younger. And there were plenty of boys up there to court 'em now that I think on it. Damn, Reese, you just dashed the dreams I was conjurin' up about those two."

There was more laughter. "Well maybe there's some others. There's got to be a couple among all those families who've come into marriageable age in the past couple years."

"Now that's something I can pin my hopes on."

Coppersmith sat back and finished off his beer.

THREE DAYS LATER, the two bounty hunters met at the livery stable. Coppersmith was saddling his horse, one of those taken from the outlaws after his own had been shot during the battle at Cedar Vale. The outlaws' other horses had been sold and the money put into the city's coffers. Milstead was, with the help of the livery owner, hitching up the jail wagon. They had decided that Milstead would take the wagon with him back into Indian Territory and hopefully fill it with outlaws worth plenty of reward money. Heading for Wichita, Coppersmith would have no need for it.

Soon both were finished, with Milstead having also tied his horse to the back of the wagon. They shook hands. "It was a pleasure ridin' with you, Reese," Coppersmith said. "Even though you snore and fart too much."

"You're just jealous that you ain't as good at 'em." He smiled. "It was good ridin' with you, too, Jace. You're a good man to have at my back when times get hard."

"Same here for you."

"And I'd be pleased to ride with you again should you take up the callin' again."

"Same here again."

"I wish you luck with findin' a fine, spirited filly up there in Wichita. Just make sure she ain't too spirted or you won't be able to handle her bein' so young as you are." He laughed and climbed onto the wagon. As Coppersmith began to ride away, Milstead yelled, "See you back in the Nations soon when those gals send you packin'." His laughter faded as Coppersmith rode on. But he laughed, too, and shook his head. He would miss Reese. The two had worked well together. But now Coppersmith had different things to think about.

Like finding a woman and making a bid at settling down. If not with the Vogel girls well, there were others. There were new families moving in all the time, but there were others already there. Like the Fassbinder girls, Heidi and Katrina, both of whom should be of marriageable age by now. Joachim Mueller's daughter, Lotte, would be too young yet, perhaps twelve or thirteen. But in a couple of years, well that would be a different story. He could afford to wait, too, as he was barely into his twenties.

There were, he was sure, girls in town, too, who might be eligible. He thought himself handsome enough to attract women. It was just a matter of finding the right ones to court—and one who could live with his past.

With such thoughts rattling around in his brain, it seemed to take forever and two days to make the trip to Wichita, but it was really only four days.

He stopped at the livery stables and left his horse after withstanding the stableman's somewhat enthusiastic greeting. Then, carrying his saddlebags and Winchester, got a room in the Wichita House. Skipping getting himself gussied up, he headed for Marshal Dan Quinn's office. As he walked down Court Street, he saw Quinn and Deputy Harry Wallace scurrying to the office and smiled. It didn't take long for word to get around that he was back.

"Well, look what the cat dragged in," Quinn said with a grin as Coppersmith entered the office.

"I've heard that before."

"Welcome back, Jace. You here to stay this time?"

"Might be. Decided to see if I can put down roots

here. Don't know if I'll be successful at it, but it's worth a try."

"Reese with you? I heard you two were partners."

"We were but we split up after a fight with some outlaws down near Cedar Vale in which we were both wounded. He more than me. I decided to try my luck at civilization. He said he had tried and failed and was goin' back to bounty huntin' on his own."

Quinn nodded. "You lookin' to get your badge back here?"

Coppersmith grinned. "Might be, but like I told Reese, maybe I'll even get to keep my deputy county sheriff's badge, if I can find the damn thing. If I do, though, I'll be your boss, Dan." He kept a bland expression on his face.

"Like hell you will," Quinn snapped angrily. "Sheriff Cartwright and you'd have charge over a much larger jurisdiction, but you wouldn't be my boss, dammit."

Coppersmith could hold back no longer, and he burst into laughter. "Of course not, Dan. Lordy but you're a touchy fella."

"Well, you'd be, too," he huffed, "if some pipsqueak tried to boss you around." But he grinned. "Got me there, Jace. Sure as hell did."

20

"HI, MR. JACE!" ANNIE SEAVER CALLED OUT TO Coppersmith.

The bounty hunter grinned wide and knelt as Annie came marching up quite ladylike. "Well, look at you, little miss. Almost all grown up. You must be twenty years old by now."

"I'm nine. And a half," Anne said indignantly.

"I was just joshin' you, Annie. But you sure are growin' up. Pretty soon you'll be of an age to marry, and by then you'll be as pretty as your ma." He stood. "Sorry to be so forward, Mrs. Seaver."

"It's Callie, as you should well know. And any woman would be pleased to be called beautiful, especially when she ain't."

"I'm not one to argue with a lady most times, but this is one time I must. What I said is true. You are a handsome woman, Callie." He looked around. But where's—" He stopped at a panicked look from Callie. He looked down at Annie and smiled. "I bet you still like penny candy even though you're practically all grown up, so would you like to get some, Miss Annie?"

"Oh, yes," the girl said, trying to keep the excitement out of her voice.

"Well, here's a nickel," he said, handing the girl a coin. "Go and get yourself something over at Mr. Carver's mercantile."

"Can I Ma, can I?"

"Yes, dear. Go on, go." When the girl had gone, Callie said, "Mort died more than a year ago."

"I'm sorry to hear that." Deep down inside he admitted only to himself that he was not really all that sorry.

"I try not to remind Annie of it as much as possible. She misses her pa."

"I imagine she would. But what are you doin' in Dodge City?"

"Looking for a fresh start, I guess you could say. A friend lives here and encouraged me to join her. I sold the farm and came away with enough that I can be comfortable for some small time while I find a way to settle myself."

"Apologizin' again for be so forward, but I'm surprised you ain't remarried. A woman as pretty and as refined as you has likely had dozens of men callin', or at least wantin' to."

Callie laughed, a delightful sound to Coppersmith. "Pretty? Well, maybe, I reckon. Not too much though. But refined? I beg to differ, sir. But it's true that several men have wanted to come calling. It took me a while to grieve for Mort. I cared for him very much. I'm over it now, as much as a widow can be, but I've not seen a man in Dodge that interests me enough to allow him to come courting me."

Coppersmith thought he saw interest in her eyes. He looked deep into those eyes, and he felt an odd sensation inside. He had faced gun-toting outlaws, hard men all, for several years now, had killed more than his share, been wounded more than once, a few times severely. None of that scared him. But saying what he wanted to say—or ask—this woman was more frightening than anything he had ever faced.

"Jace?" Callie said, a little worriedly. "Jace, are you all right?"

Coppersmith grinned ruefully. "Sorry, Callie, my mind wandered there for a bit while I wrestled with something in my head. I was gonna ask—"

Annie came running up, cutting him off. "Look, Ma, licorice."

"That's good dear," Callie said, wondering herself now what had been on Coppersmith's mind. But she put that aside. "What are *you* doing in Dodge? Searchin' for more outlaws?"

"Sadly, yes. As always. This time legally, though. He opened his jacket to show the star on his chest. I'm a deputy sheriff in Sedgwick County."

"Well, I am impressed, Jace. A deputy sheriff!"

"It ain't all it might be cracked up to be. Much of it is deadly." He laughed. "Deadly boring that is. There is the occasional outlaw or gang to chase down after a robbery or something."

"Is that what you're doing in Dodge? It's a far piece from Wichita, which is in Sedgwick County, I believe."

"That it is. I'm here to talk to a Mr. George Hinkle, sheriff of Ford County, about some outlaws who appeared to be headed this way after robbing a bank in Park City."

"I hope you catch them."

"Me, too."

"Well, I must be going," Callie said, reluctance touching her voice. "It was nice to see you again, Jace. Perhaps we can see each other again before you head back to Wichita?"

"That would be nice, ma'am," he responded rather forlornly. As Callie walked away, he cursed himself silently for not having had the courage to talk to her about what he wanted to. He sighed. Maybe some other time, he thought.

He turned with hope springing into his chest when Callie called to him, then hurried up. "What about Travis?" she asked almost breathlessly, crushing his hope.

"What about him?"

"I don't mean Travis, really. Well, I do hope he's all right. But the little girl. Is she all right? Was she found? Is she safe?"

Coppersmith smiled. "She's safe, being raised by another German family. Friends of the family who had acted as her parents. They were her grandparents actually. She was tired and hungry and dirty when I found—um, when she was found—but otherwise all right.

"What little girl, Ma?" Anne asked.

"Never mind. I'll tell you about it later." She looked squarely at Coppersmith. "So *you* found her?"

"Well others were lookin' for her too and—"

"I bet her rescue was not easy."

He grinned crookedly. "Easier than one might have figured, but still—" he glanced down at Annie, then back at the girl's mother "—messy, shall we say."

"Thank the Lord you saved her."

"Who is this girl?" Annie insisted.

Coppersmith knelt again so he would be eye to eye

with her. "She's a friend of mine. Like you are. A beautiful girl, just like you. She's a little younger than you. Her name is Lizette."

"That's a pretty name. Can I meet her? We could play together."

"Maybe someday, Annie." He stood. "And Travis has been cleared of all wrongdoing, though it took some doing to get that straightened out."

"That's good," Callie said dispassionately. "Now we really must go. My friend is waiting for us. Will you meet us for lunch tomorrow?" Callie blushed.

"I would be delighted," Coppersmith said, almost stumbling over the words in his newfound awkwardness.

"Quigley's restaurant."

"I'll be there."

———

FROM THE CORNER of his eyes, Coppersmith couldn't tell if Callie was bemused or annoyed that he had been spending much of their time at the meal talking to Annie. He didn't like that he was to a large degree ignoring Callie, but he couldn't seem to help it. He didn't know what to say to her, how to act toward her. He had never dealt with a woman like this before. Missy Birch had been shy but had a wild side that came raging out when they were intimate; Lily was too innocent for him to be too forward with, at least until they were married, which of course, he had ruined any possibility of. He had not gotten close to either of the Vogel girls, but there was Helena Hoffner, who while innocent yet was beginning to edge into a little rebelliousness against her parents, something that might bode well for Coppersmith. But Callie was different. She was a woman, a full-grown one, not one barely of marriageable age. She was a full-figured woman who had been married and birthed a daughter, yet still youthful. She was neither innocent nor, as far as he could tell, wanton. He believed, or maybe just wanted to believe, that she was lusty and would be a willing partner in a marriage bed.

But it all added up to a nervous time at lunch, so he had concentrated on entertaining Anne.

As they finished, Callie said, a bit tightly, Coppersmith thought, "You will escort us home, of course, Jace." It was not a question.

"Yes, ma'am."

Outside, Callie hooked an arm through his, surprising him. Annie took his other hand, and they strode down the street, Callie nodding greetings to a number of people, both men and women. It made Coppersmith all the more uneasy.

At their house, on the porch, Callie said, "Annie, go on in the house. Jace and I have some things to discuss."

"But, Ma—"

"Do as your mother says," Coppersmith ordered gently. "I'll say goodbye to you for now and tell you we'll see each other again. I promise."

"All right." The girl flounced inside.

When the girl was inside, Callie turned to face Coppersmith. "Have I done something to offend you, Jace?" she asked.

"No, of course not," he responded, startled.

"Are you embarrassed to be seen with me?"

"No, ma'am, I'm honored."

"It certainly doesn't seem that way."

"What do you mean?" Coppersmith's nervousness returned in full force.

"You spent most of lunch taking with Annie instead

of me and you seemed to be mighty tense when I took your arm walking back here. It leads me to believe that you have no, shall we say, feelings toward me. At least not good ones."

"It ain't that. It's just... I can't... I..." He hung his head and almost shuffled his feet like a ten-year-old caught with his hand in the cookie jar.

"You're afraid to talk to me?" Callie asked, caught between anger and astonishment.

"Yes," the lawman said quietly.

"How many men have you killed, Jace?"

His head snapped up. "That's a hell of a question to ask a man, beggin' your pardon for my language."

"It's been more than a few, I suppose."

"It has," Coppersmith almost spat, anger replacing the anxiety. "And I'm sorry if I've offended you by bein' such a rabid killer in your eyes. I apologize and will not bother you again." He turned to leave.

"Jace," she called gently. He turned. "I didn't ask because I want to know a number or because I'm offended by what you have been called to do. I asked because it takes a lot of courage to kill a man, especially when you've faced many dangers in doing so. Yet here you are afraid to talk to me? I find that strange. If you'd rather not speak to me, have the courage to say so. I will be hurt but I will accept it."

"But I—"

"And if you want to talk to me, do so. You're a brave man, Jace Coppersmith. You should have no fear of talking to a simple woman."

"You ain't simple. And I've never met a woman like you."

"Is that good or bad?" She smiled gently.

"Good, of course."

"What about that woman you were planning to marry back in Colorado Territory?"

"She was young, flighty sometimes. You... I ain't sure how to treat you."

"Why?" Callie asked, eyebrows raised in surprise.

"You're a woman. A real woman, not some fickle girl. I've never been close to a real woman."

"You've never been close to a woman?" Again she was incredulous.

"That ain't what I mean. I've been close to women, but most were young or of loose morals. And my ma, well she wasn't much of a woman, or a mother. But you, well, you're a high-class woman, one who's special."

Callie laughed. "Now I think you've lost your reason, Jace. I'm nothing special, nor am I high class. I'm just a plain old woman."

"Now it's my turn to argue again," Coppersmith said, losing a considerable amount of indecisiveness. "You're not plain, and you certainly ain't old."

"I'm a lot older than you." Much of the joy in her voice had faded.

"If it doesn't bother me, it shouldn't bother you."

"You don't care that I'm older than you and have been a married woman three times over?"

"Nope."

"Or that I have a daughter?"

"Annie is a delightful child."

"You don't know my background."

"Nor do you know mine. I know you've been married before. What else happened ain't my concern."

"It might be if you heard."

"And learnin' of my background likely will offend you."

"You've been a bounty hunter and a lawman and have

killed quite a few men, all for justice. That's all I need to know."

Coppersmith pulled himself up, once again feeling strong and confident. "So you're sayin' you'd like me to court you?"

"Yes," Callie said and blushed.

"I'd be privileged to come callin' on you, Callie, but it's a far piece between here and Wichita."

"We'll find a way, I'm sure," Callie looked left and right to make sure no one was paying attention to them, then quickly kissed him on the lips, startling them both a little. She blushed again.

Then came a cheering voice from inside the house.

"Annie Seaver, you may find yourself on the wrong end of a switch, young lady."

"I'm sorry, Mama."

"You don't sound like it."

But she and Coppersmith laughed.

21

COPPERSMITH WAS STROLLING DOWN CHISHOLM Street near the courthouse when he and Van Horn spotted each other. They approached carefully and stopped a couple yards apart.

"Howdy, Travis," the former said.

"Jace."

"Been in town long?"

"Long enough. Why're you askin'."

Coppersmith shrugged. "Just chattin' with a former friend."

"Former?"

"You weren't exactly friendly last time we saw each other."

"That's 'cause you and my brother were annoyin' sons of bitches."

The younger man gritted his teeth, then relaxed to say, "Annoyin' only in your mind, Travis. Unless you call tryin' to talk some sense into you annoyin'."

"Like hell. Where is my brother anyway?"

"Down in the Nations, I expect."

"You don't know?"

"Nope. Why should I?"

"You two were thick as peas in a pod last I saw."

"We were just friendly is all. I left both of you one mornin' before you two woke up if you'll remember. About a year later, Reese and I teamed up to hunt men down in the Nations, then I decided to try to settle down."

"So you picked Wichita? Why? So you can get that star I see on your chest?"

"Yep. When I was contemplatin' this, I figured Dan would rehire me and maybe Sheriff Cartwright would keep me on as a deputy. I decided to stick with Cartwright. Besides, there's the Germans."

"What about 'em?"

"Friendly folk. Appreciative of things people, even you, do for 'em." Despite his simmering anger, he managed a smile. "Some fine young women to court, too."

Van Horn just grunted.

"What're you doin' back in Wichita, Travis? I thought you'd stay away."

"I do most of the time, but I was nearby and decided to stop and maybe see some old friends. Well, used to be friends. Nobody seems friendly anymore. I reckon the city is changin' and folks with it."

"The city ain't changed, Travis, it's you who changed. Gone from a decent, honorable man to... hell, I don't even know what you are these days."

"I'm the same fella I always was."

"No, you ain't. You've been a different man—a changed man, for the worse—ever since you got it in your head that you wanted to be a father to that little girl who you didn't even know. She needed—still needs—a real family. Not some footloose man hunter who has no roots anywhere."

"She's my daughter, dammit."

"As Reese and I told you more than a couple years ago, and as I just told you, you're not her father, and she ain't your daughter. She was the Bassmyers' child, and now she's the Muellers'." Coppersmith had a sudden unease. "You ain't come back here to do something concernin' that child, have you?" he asked urgently.

"And if I do?"

"Travis, do not even think about doin' anything concerning her."

"And if I do?" Van Horn repeated, this time with a sneer.

"I will kill you, Travis. Do not doubt that even the least littlest bit. I will put a bullet in that empty skull of yours."

"You ain't got the ability or the stones."

"Understand me, Travis. If you go near that girl other than a friendly visit to her parents—that's the Muellers— I will kill you, no hesitation, no thought that you used to be a friend, and the man who taught me everything about bein' an honorable man."

"You can't take me. Like you said, I taught you everything, and I'm still better than you."

"Unless you backshoot me, I don't think you are, but I'd rather not find out. But believe me when I say I'll kill you. If I die in the doin', so be it. I'd rather go down in a gunfight killin' you than let you get your hands on Lizette."

"Just get outta my way." Van Horn shoved past Coppersmith, hitting his shoulder as he did.

The latter turned, ready to pound the former, then decided it was not worth it, but he decided that he would keep an eye on Travis Van Horn as long as the bounty hunter was in town. Then he decided that he would also keep an eye on him until Van Horn left the county.

"I'LL HAVE some of my deputies keep an eye on Travis when he's in town. You can't do it all the time," Wichita Marshal Dan Quinn said.

Coppersmith nodded. "I doubt he'll do anything in town, but it's good to watch over him. Maybe Hector can help me keep an eye on him 'til he's out of the county. Sheriff Cartwright shouldn't object."

"Best watch over the Muellers even after he leaves the county. He'll likely know, or at least suspect he's bein' watched and might double back after he leaves Sedgwick County."

"Good idea, Dan."

"YOU CAN'T SHADOW me forever, Jace," Van Horn said as the two men sat side by side on horseback. A roiling expanse of fertile farmland in full bloom stretched out before them, with the Mueller house not far away in front of them.

"That's a fact," Coppersmith said. "But I ain't alone, and I'll shadow you as much as I can. Others will take over when I can't."

"And how long will you do this?"

"Long as you're in the county. If you leave and come back, I'll be on your tail again. I will not let you harm Lizette. That is the truest fact you will ever hear, for if you do, you will forfeit your life no matter how long it takes, no matter how far you run. I will consider you takin' her from her family—"

"The Muellers ain't her family."

"Yes, they are. More than you have been and more than you'll ever hope to be. And if you take her from her family, I will consider it harmin' her, as she was taken from her parents once before and it'll damage her mind forever if it happens again, especially by someone she doesn't know."

"She knows—"

"Like hell, Travis. You've got to get over this idea that you can somehow be a father to that girl. You have a job that keeps you on the trail ninety percent of your time huntin' outlaws, much of it in Indian Territory, which is practically ruled by outlaws. You want a daughter to be there? Reese told me about Kate and her son. You want that for Lizette?"

"Well no, but—"

"Would you still take her there with you? That'd be a great life for a seven-year-old. Lordy how can you be so stupid, Travis? I've never seen you like this before."

"I never had a daughter before."

"You don't have a daughter now, dammit. Not really." Coppersmith sighed in annoyance with Van Horn's recalcitrance. "You will never be a father—a real father—to that child. At best you can hope to be something of an uncle. And you can only do that if you settle down, find a job that doesn't entail chasin' outlaws, get married, and slowly start takin' part in her life, as much as the Muellers will allow. And that might be damn little considerin' everything else."

"I was married here once, Jace."

"I know that, and I know what happened, at least some of it. Lizette was born of that marriage, but with the life you've led since, you have no claim to that girl. It's a mighty sad thing that Gretchen died. It's even sadder that you weren't with her to comfort her in her last hours. But even if you had, you'd have had no way to raise a newborn. You wouldn't go out and get married again the next day, You'd have to have had the Bassmyers take her in, at least for a while, and you'd go back to bounty huntin'. That'd put you right back where you are now."

"I could've settled down again, like I had with Gretchen. Find a new wife after a bit, and we could raise Lizette."

"Are you certain? And if you did marry again, would your wife want to raise a child not her own, who she was not related to, one who was just born? Maybe. Maybe not. But if things didn't go right, again you'd be back where you are now."

"You once told me—and I hear you've told others— that I not only taught you to be a man hunter but also to be a man. An honorable man you said."

"It's true, even though you threw it back in my face."

"One of the many thousand things I've done wrong in my life, Jace. But I will say this—you have turned into a good man, an honorable man, a decent man." He looked out over the corn waving in the breeze. "But that's something I seem to have lost, Jace. I got my mind so intent on takin' care of Lizette that I can't think with any reason. I've stayed away a while, yet knowin' she's here pulled me back."

"Leave her be, Travis. Just leave her be. Let her be a little girl, in a carin' family, with brothers and sisters to play with and care for her."

Van Horn sat for a while, staring out over the fields with blank eyes. Then he turned his gaze to Copper-

172 | JOHN LEGG

smith, who saw that his companion had a sad, weary look to the eyes. "Think I might could see her one last time?"

"If the Muellers allow it, which they should. They don't know what an ass you've been about all this. The other thing is, I go with you."

"You don't trust me?"

"No." Coppersmith got no pleasure of the flash of anger in Van Horn's eyes.

"All right, let's go."

They rode down to the house. As they neared, Coppersmith called, "Joachim! Ingrid! Visitors."

"Mueller will be home?"

"Noon meal."

The Muellers stepped out onto the porch. "Jace, Travis," Mueller said happily, coming down off the porch to shake their hands when they dismounted.

The children pushed their way past their parents. Lizette saw Coppersmith, and her face lit up. "Mr. Jace!" She rushed up and jumped into his arms as he knelt.

He rose, picking her up. "My you're gettin' to be a big girl. Soon you'll be as big as your mother. And maybe prettier." He winked at Ingrid.

"See, *Liebling*," Mueller said. "The girls vill be prettier than you, und the boys vill be more handsome than their papa."

Lizette giggled and rubbed her cheek against one of Coppersmith's. Then she pulled back a little. "You face is scratchy," she admonished.

"Well, maybe I'm growin' a beard like your papa. Or maybe I'm just too lazy to shave," he said with a laugh.

Suddenly Van Horn jumped on his horse and galloped away. Everyone stood watching him fade into the horizon.

"Vhat vas that?" Ingrid asked.

"I think he just remembered he had urgent business in town."

"He didn't say hello," Lizette complained. "That's rude. I've seen him two times, I think, but he doesn't stay long."

"Yes, it's rude, and he feels uncomfortable around pretty young girls." He forced a smile onto his face. "I'll tell you hello from him. He just wasn't thinkin'." He set the girl down. "You folks all right?" he asked, though it was plain to see that his mind was drifting elsewhere.

"Ya. Is goot. The children, they are goot, too." Mueller's eyes flicked to the speck in the distance that was Travis Van Horn. "Go, *mein Freund*."

Coppersmith nodded once, hurriedly climbed into the saddle and took off. He pulled up alongside Van Horn, who had stopped along the stream that watered Mueller's crops and those of several neighbors.

"You son of a bitch," Van Horn snapped. He looked as if he were going for one of the revolvers.

"Don't do that, Travis," Coppersmith said, resting a hand on the butt of one Colt. "Now what's in your craw."

"You bastard, stealin' my daughter from me."

22

"Damn, here we go again. How'd I do that?" Coppersmith took his hand away from his six-gun when Van Horn did the same.

"I saw the way she looked so happy when she saw you. She didn't look at me that way."

"She didn't look at you at all. Because she hadn't gotten around to it. She would have in a minute. She's a child, Travis. They get excited and do one thing at a time sometimes."

"And the hug she gave you."

"I see her fairly often. I try to stop by and see her sometimes."

"See what I mean?"

"No. Look, she likes me because I rescued her, and because I visit sometimes." Seeing Van Horn's fresh look of annoyance, he added, "I don't come out here just to see her, Travis. I was courtin' Helena Hoffner. When I came out here to see Helena, I'd often stopped by the Muellers. If you had waited another minute or two, she would've greeted you. She remembers you but as a friend of the family, not as her friend like I am. If you had acted normally, maybe she could've become your friend, too, eventually."

"I blundered again, didn't I?"

"In a big way, Travis. The best thing I can tell you now is to ride on out and not come back. Forget about Lizette."

"Gonna be hard to do."

"I imagine it will. But you've done hard things before."

"None this hard."

Coppersmith nodded.

"Reckon you're right. I'll just ride on. You gonna follow me?"

"Do I have to?"

"No."

"I have your word?"

"Yep, for what it's worth."

"It's still worth a lot to me, Travis." He held out his hand.

After a few moments hesitation, Van Horn took it. Without another word, he turned and trotted off.

Coppersmith sat and watched for a couple of minutes, then turned and headed back to the Muellers' house.

The family heard him arrive and they all came out again.

"Everyt'ink all right?" Mueller asked.

"As much as it can be. He has—" he paused "—business elsewhere that'll keep him away for a long time."

The Mueller parents nodded.

Coppersmith took a deep breath and let it out slowly, calming himself and working up a smile. "Hey, little Miss Lizette, do you want to take a ride."

"Oh, yes. Can I, Papa?"

"She is not so little for sitting in front of you on the saddle, Jace," Mueller said nervously after a moment's thought.

Coppersmith nodded, but before he could say anything, Ingrid laid a hand on her husband's arm. "It vill be all right, Joachim. It vill be the last time, though, yah?" She looked at Coppersmith, who smiled sadly.

"I'll miss such rides but you're right."

"I can't ride with Mr. Jace no more?" Lizette asked, close to tears."

"No you can't, *Schatzi*—Treasure," Ingrid said. You are gettink to be big girl now and big girl's ridin' like that is improper. So this vill be the last time."

"Well, little one, let's enjoy it," Coppersmith said with something of a forced smile. He reached down, grabbed her and swung her onto the saddle in front of him. "We won't be long," he said and ambled off.

Once out of sight of the house, Coppersmith handed the reins to Lizette. As they rode slowly past another cornfield, he mused, more then said, "Maybe I can talk your ma and pa into lettin' you ride your own horse."

Lizette jerked her head around, eyes wide, to look at him. "You will?"

"Well, all I can do is ask, but I'll do that. I don't know that they'll agree, though, so don't hope too much."

"All right, Herr Jace," she said, happily remembering her German despite her excitement. She faced front again.

He laughed. "So you're learnin' German, are you?"

"Yah. It's funny sometimes." She chuckled. "But Mama and Papi say I must learn."

"It's a good thing. You listen to them and learn as well as you can."

"I will." Lizette suddenly turned her head around to look at him again, this time with sadness in her eyes. "Will you still come to see me if I can't ride with you?"

"Of course I will. You're my most favorite girl in the whole world."

"But I heard Mama and Papi say you see Fräulein Hoffner. Maybe you like her more than me."

"Well, I liked her in a different way but not more. And I don't see her anymore. Even if I did, you'd still be my favorite girl. But you're too young for me to spend too much time with you."

"I don't understand. I'm too old to ride with you but too young to be with you more?"

"Yep, that's about it. Strange, ain't it? But you'll understand when you get older. Someday, oh, in nine or ten years maybe, you'll find a boy your age and will maybe want to get married."

"But I—"

Coppersmith knew what she was going to say and needed to head it off. "Hush, now, Lizette. You'll understand as you get older. Just remember, you'll always be special to me."

She stared at him for a few moments, then turned her head back so she was looking forward again. "All right," she said, sounding both curious and dejected.

———

"I THINK you should let me teach the children to ride, Joachim," Coppersmith said when he and Lizette returned to the house."

"*Nein*," Ingrid said before her husband could respond. "*Der Kinder* don't need to know how to ride a horse. *Nein*."

"Ah, *Liebling*, vhat could it hurt?"

"It could hurt the children. They may fall off, hurt themselves, break their bones. *Nein*. You haf *mein* answer, Herr Coppersmith."

Mueller shrugged. "Frau Mueller has answered."

The lawman nodded, but he thought he saw some mischief in Mueller's eyes.

———

A WEEK LATER, about the time Mueller and his children would be at home for nooning, Coppersmith rode up to the house driving three horses, saddled and bridled. He stopped in front of the house, dismounted, and tied the animals to the hitching rail.

"Vot is this, Herr Coppersmith?" Ingrid demanded.

"Horses for—"

"I told you, *nein*. I vill not have it."

"Now, now, *Liebchen*," Mueller said, placing a beefy arm around his wife's strong shoulders. "They vant to do this, and Herr Coppersmith will teach them vell. He vill vatch out for them."

"I don't like it, Joachim," Ingrid said and stomped into the house.

"I hope I haven't caused you much trouble, Joachim."

"I think she vill come around." He grinned. "Unless one of the children gets thrown to the ground and is hurt."

"I'll try not to let that happen. All right, Karl, this is yours." He pointed to a smallish, but full-grown chestnut. "His name's Chub. Now come on, up you go." He helped the young teenager into the saddle, then adjusted the length of the stirrups.

"Now you, Gisela." He helped the twelve-year-old

into the saddle on the even smaller full-grown horse and adjusted the stirrups. "Her name's Betsy."

"And now your turn, Lizette." The girl was fairly bouncing with excitement. The bay pony waited patiently as Lisette was helped aboard and things adjusted. "Her name's Glory."

"That's a pretty name."

"Yep." Coppersmith patiently showed the two Mueller children how to use the reins. Lizette sat, fidgety. She wanted to ride. Finally, Coppersmith mounted his bay gelding and rode off with Lizette on his left, Gisela to her left and Karl on Coppersmith's right. The deputy sheriff once again surprised himself with his patience in dealing with the children.

After an hour, the Mueller children were getting saddle sore. Lisette was more used to being in the saddle for long periods so didn't suffer much. At the house, Coppersmith helped them off the animals, the children headed for the house.

"Whoa, there young ones," Coppersmith said. "Now comes the not so fun part." Under Ingrid's glare, he walked his bay into the barn while the children did so with theirs.

For the next hour, Coppersmith taught the children how to unsaddle the animals and safely store the tack, care for the horses, the importance of making sure they had food and water. Then he showed them how to saddle their horses. Gisela and especially Lizette needed help doing so.

Finally, they headed to the house, the children bubbling with excitement despite their sore posteriors. Ingrid's frosty glare began to melt just a little when she saw the children's enthusiasm.

"You vill stay for supper, Jace, yah?"

He grinned. "Is it safe for me to be in the house where you have ready access to knives and hot pans and such?"

"Yah." She grinned just a little. "Maybe."

"I'll wait outside till Joachim gets back." He sat on a rocking chair on the porch. A vision of living in such a place with a loving family around him floated before his eyes. The mind picture was pleasing to him. But he worried it was out of reach.

He was still sitting there when Joachim returned. "You are vaiting for supper?" the German asked.

"Yep. I was afraid to go inside where Ingrid has knives and cleavers and such."

Mueller laughed. "Come, I vill protect you, me and the children."

Coppersmith laughed also, and the two men went inside.

Supper started off uncomfortably but soon became more friendly. Ingrid's iciness melted a little more under the delighted talk of the children about the day's experiences.

"Well, that was a fine meal, Mrs. Mueller. Unless you poisoned my portion." He tried to keep a straight face.

"I might, Mr. Coppersmith," she said icily, "next time you utter such a remark. And now I must ask you to leave."

Instead of a grin or laugh, Coppersmith grimaced. What was supposed to be a joke had turned black. "Ingrid," he said apologetically, "that was wrong for me to say. I meant it as a joke. It was, I realized too late, no such thing. Just so you know, I would be more apt to poison myself than worry about you doing it. Thank you for the meal. Children, make sure the horses are cared for." He grabbed his hat from a peg beside the door and left, cursing himself for being such a fool.

As he was getting ready to mount his horse, Lizette came flying out of the house. "Don't go, Jace. Don't—"

"Get back here, young lady," Ingrid shouted from inside and a moment later was on the porch also. "Go inside, Lizette."

"No." The girl dodged her mother. "I want Jace to stay."

"Lizette!" Coppersmith bellowed. When the girl stopped and looked at him wide-eyed in worry, he said softly, "A young lady does not disobey her ma. Nor does she run away from her ma, especially when she's done something wrong. Now you go back in the house with your mother and take whatever punishment she gives you."

"But—"

"Do not argue, young lady. I will be back in a couple days to get the horses. Your ma didn't want you ridin' them, and now I expect I'll not be welcome back here— except to get the animals. I'm sorry I won't be able to teach you anymore, but it's my fault and you children will, sadly, have to pay for it." He mounted Pard. "Just remember, obey your ma and pa." He yanked the gelding's head around much harder than usual and galloped off. "Damn fool," he muttered over and over.

———

TWO DAYS LATER, Coppersmith stopped in front of the house, dismounted, and tied the bay to the hitching rail. He stepped onto the porch and called through the screen door, "Ingrid, it's Jace. I've come to take the horses back. I just wanted to let you know lest you think some horse

thieves were around." He stepped off the porch and
headed for the barn. He stopped and turned when Ingrid
called to him.

"I don't know if I can ever forgive you, Jace. But it is
not fair that *der kinder* pay for it. You may leave the
horses and come for two hours every three days to teach
the children.

"Yes'm."

23

"I KNOW, THIS IS BECOMING A HABIT," Coppersmith said as he laid his badge on Sheriff Baxter Cartwright's desk.

"Something wrong, Jace?" Cartwright asked, surprised. He did not like the look of sadness on Coppersmith's face.

"No. I just decided it was time to mosey on."

Cartwright still gazed at him in concern for some moments before saying, "I don't believe you, Jace." He held up a hand to stop the now former lawman from saying anything. "But that's your business. That badge'll be here whenever—if ever—you want it again."

"Thanks, Baxter. I appreciate it." He left and headed toward Marshal Dan Quinn's office. Along the way, he had a youth track the lawman down and tell him to meet Coppersmith at the office. Coppersmith was leaning against the wall next to the door when Quinn hurried up.

"What's up, Jace?" he asked.

"I'll tell you inside, Dan."

Quinn looked at him in surprise and shook his head as he unlocked the door. "Sit," he said.

"I'll stand. I won't be here long."

"That sounds ominous."

"It might be, depending on how you look at it." He paused almost grinning at the confusion on Quinn's face. "I'm leavin' Wichita, Dan."

"Why in hell...? Have you told Sheriff...? He stopped, pointing to Coppersmith's shirt, where the badge had been shortly before. "Told him already, eh?"

"Yep."

"Again, why?

"It's time."

"What about Helena?"

"I thought you knew. I haven't courted her in a long time."

"Nope, didn't know.

"What about Lizette? That girl adores you, Jace."

"I know." The sadness in his face deepened.

Quinn's hand inched toward his revolver. "You didn't do anything to that girl, did you?" His voice was harsh.

"Of course not," Coppersmith replied, surprised. "I'd shoot myself in the head before I did anything untoward to that girl."

The marshal relaxed, some. "I figured, but I had to ask. I still don't understand it."

Coppersmith shrugged. "Ain't much to understand, Dan. I just figure it's time to move on." He would not tell Quinn about his falling out with Ingrid Mueller.

"But you—" Quinn stopped, took a deep breath, and nodded. "You'll be missed, Jace. Both as a dependable lawman who was a big help more than once, but more important as a friend. You'll always be welcome here, with a badge or without."

"I appreciate it Dan." He held out his hand.

Quinn shook it but at the same time said, "You best make sure you say goodbye to Lizette."

"I will," he lied. Coppersmith turned and left. He got his gear from the room where he had been staying, saddled his horse at the livery stable and rode to the train terminal. Two hours later, he boarded the train, with his bay in a stock car.

As the train pulled out of the station, Coppersmith stared glumly out the window. Though he could not see it in reality, in his mind's eye he could see the Bassmyers' place, now owned by their oldest son, and the Mueller place. And he envisioned the latter at a better time, with a smiling Ingrid and a happy Joachim, but most of all, a bouncy, excited, joyful despite all that had happened to her, Lizette. "Goodbye, Lizette," he whispered, sadness sticking to him like a cactus needle embedded deep in his skin but far more painful. It would be even more painful, he thought, when he saw Annie Seaver, as she greeted him with an excited "Mr. Jace!" the exact same way Lizette did.

It was late in the day when he arrived in Dodge City. He stabled his horse, found a room, and had himself a good meal. In the morning, with a heavy dose of trepidation roiling inside him, he headed for the house near Cedar Street and Avenue B. He hesitated for some moments before he knocked on the door.

Callie Seaver opened the door and her eyes widened in surprise. "Jace!" she gasped.

It seemed to Coppersmith that she had been expecting someone else, but he said, "Callie. How are—"

"Mr. Jace!" Annie yelled and came barreling past her mother and bounced happily in front of Coppersmith. He knelt. "My you're lookin' like a fine young lady, Miss Annie. It's been a time since I saw you."

"Too long," Annie admonished him with a light, tinkling laugh.

"I think you're right.

"It's not been so long since—"

"Go back inside now, Annie!" Callie snapped.

The girl, a little shocked at her mother's tone, went meekly back inside.

"I'm sorry, Jace. I believe she was about to say something she shouldn't." She sighed. "I'd invite you in but having a single man in my house would be unseemly."

"I know, Callie. I just wanted to ask if you'd accompany to lunch this afternoon."

"I... I don't know, Jace. I—"

Coppersmith nodded. "I see. There's someone else in your life now." It was a statement not a question.

"Yes," the woman whispered. "You hadn't come in such a long time—months—that I thought you had abandoned... had forgotten about me, that you'd found someone else. So when... someone asked to come calling, I said yes. It was a difficult decision, considering the circumstances."

"Mind tellin' me who this gent is?" Coppersmith was unsuccessful at keeping the anger out of his voice.

"That would be inappropriate, especially since I figure there's a good chance you would look for him and perhaps try to do him harm."

"You really think that I'd do something like that?"

"No, but I fear you would. I also fear that you would be harmed."

"That's a foolish notion. Ain't many as good as I am. But I'm not one to stay where I'm not wanted. I'll be in Dodge for a while. Don't know how long yet, though not

as long as I had been plannin'." He smiled sadly. "But if I
see you around town, I'll not bother you. Or your new
beau if he's with you." He paused to clear his throat of
the clogged feeling that had grown there. "Bye, Callie.
Tell Annie goodbye for me and that I'll miss her."

"I will." Her voice was barely above a whisper, and
there was a more than a hint of sorrow in her words.

COPPERSMITH WISHED that Callie lived closer to the
center of town, where it was crowded as people shopped
and conducted business. Had she done so, he could've
kept a watch on her place to see who her new suitor was
and then perhaps talk to the man and impress upon him
the need to find someone else to court.

But she lived in an area where there were only houses
offering no real protection for spying on her. So he spent
some time lounging around outside of one business or
another, or wandering aimlessly about the town,
watching for her.

Over the next several weeks, he saw Callie and Annie
frequently as she went about her business. But Annie
was her only companion.

As time went by, he began to wonder if she had lied
to him, hinting that there was another caller because she
just did not want Coppersmith to come around anymore.
More than once he considered trying to talk to her,
explaining that law business had kept him away for all
those months. For a short time, he had flirted with
Helena Hoffner, but he was not seriously pursuing her.
He did it to have female companionship of a sort, and he
thought she knew that despite likely hoping it would
turn into more. But his mind had always been on Callie,

and for the first few months he was able to catch a train and visit her now and again for a few days. But as the months passed, he could never seem to find the time to get away long enough to make the trip to Dodge despite wanting to. There was always another outlaw to chase or prisoner to be escorted to the capital, Topeka, or a convicted felon to be taken to the state prison in Lansing.

So it had come to this. It made him all the angrier that he had given up a badge again to spend his time with Callie.

He also loitered around town at night, stopping outside a saloon to watch for her after he had visited the establishment or before going in. But she never appeared, and after a few weeks he began to consider going back to Wichita. He could easily get his old job back, but it was getting tiresome to him to be giving up a star with some regularity for various reasons. And returning to Wichita would to him be like being a dog who had strayed and was returning home with its tail between its legs. The thought roiled Coppersmith's stomach.

But most of all, there was the main reason he left—not seeing Lizette because of her mother having banned Coppersmith from her home. Even the arrangement with teaching the children to ride had fallen by the wayside, in part because of his duties as a deputy county sheriff. Being that close to Lizette without being able to visit the child would tear at him. He was a man strong of will and spirit, but he did not think he was that strong. He had realized that, and so had turned in his badge and left Wichita.

Now his plan to be with Callie was in tatters, and he was both sickened and angered by it.

He also considered taking a position with the police

force in Dodge City or perhaps with the Ford County Sheriff's Office. Sheriff George Hinkle had approached him with just such an offer, and there were times when he seriously considered it.

But he could not bring himself to do it, and after some time he began strongly considering leaving Dodge and going back to bounty hunting. He was very good at it, and any effort he had made at settling down, however rare and halfhearted, had not worked out for him.

He was beginning to resign himself to the fact that he would be forever a bounty hunter and a man alone. But he stuck around longer, always hoping that he could find out who Callie's beau was and scare him off so Coppersmith could begin courting her himself once more.

Then, in the dimness of the oil lamps along Front Street, he saw her with her escort, and his blood froze in shock. Then it boiled over in rage. He started to head that way to challenge the man but decided not to do so in front of the crowd headed to the opera house for a play. Instead, he waited 'til he saw her the next day coming out of a milliner's store. He walked up to her.

Callie stopped, shocked. "You told me you wouldn't bother me, Jace," she accused him nervously.

"I didn't, until what I saw last night."

She blanched.

"How could you, Callie? Travis Van Horn? A man who deserted you? How could you allow him to start courtin' you?"

"I told you once a few years ago that I still harbored feelings for him. When I thought you had cast me over, and he showed up in Dodge, he appealed to me to give him another chance. I thought I'd do so, to allow him to try to make good on the love he had for me all those years ago."

"And what about me?"

"You abandoned me, too, Jace. At least that's the way it seemed. Not only did you not come to court me like you did the first few months, you never wrote or even sent a wire to let me know you were still interested in me. What was I supposed to think? It was almost as bad as when Travis first—"

"But, Callie—"

"Jace, I loved you. Well, I still do. I saw something special in you when we first met, and more so when we met again in Cottonwood Crossing. Had you continued to come calling from Wichita, even if infrequently as you did at first, I could have been yours. But when you didn't and Travis came along and apologized for the past and swore he would never leave me again, I, well I fell in love with him all over again."

"We'll just see about that." Coppersmith started to leave but turned back when Callie spoke.

"Don't do anything, Jace. Please."

"I can't let him—"

"Do you really think that if you kill him, which is obvious you want to do, that I would become yours? Surely you're not that stupid."

Coppersmith hung his head in defeat. "You're right now that I think about it." His head came back up, and there was hope in his voice when he asked, "Would it be all right if I courted you, too? Challenge him for your love that way?"

"I don't know, Jace. If you two see each other and or learn that the other is courting me, there will be gunplay, I'm sure, and one of you will be hurt if not killed." She sighed. "This is a predicament for me, Jace. I love you. I love Travis, too. Knowing that you would try to kill each other makes me ill, makes me want to cast aside both of you. But I can't. My heart won't let me." Tears were starting to make tracks down her cheeks. "It's gone too far, Jace. Leave it be."

"I'll try, Callie, I really will, but I don't know if I'll be able."

"Then leave Dodge. Go back to Wichita and take up your badge again. Or go back to bounty hunting. Just leave me be, Jace. Please."

"I was ready to settle down here, Callie. I can get a job as a lawman here. What is Travis gonna do?"

"I don't know, Jace. I don't know." She pushed her way past him.

He took a step toward following her but stopped. Chasing after her now, this way, would be a sure way to not regain her affection. Morose and angry, he strode away.

24

COPPERSMITH AND VAN HORN STOOD FACE TO face barely ten feet apart.

"What're you doin' in Dodge, Jace?" Van Horn asked with an edge to his voice.

Coppersmith almost grinned. "I could ask the same of you. But no matter. I came back to court Callie again."

Van Horn laughed. "Again?"

"Yep."

"Where'd you ever get the notion she'd want you?"

"We were courtin' and doin' fine but law business kept me from makin' it here too often. Like a fool, when I wasn't able to get here for some months, I didn't write to let her know I still loved her and still wanted her."

"Your loss, Jace. Besides, I heard you were courtin' some gal over in Wichita."

"That was a while ago, and I was just toyin' with her 'til I could get back here to Callie."

"Like I said, it's your loss. Callie's mine, boy. While you were teasin' that young filly in Wichita—one of the German girls, I'd wager—I showed up here and found

Callie. Didn't know she was here. I just come into town one day to get some supplies, have a good meal and such when I spotted her."

"And she just accepted you back in her life?"

"No, of course not. She didn't want anything to do with me at first, but I persisted. You know how I can be when I put my mind to something. And I put my mind into gettin' Callie back. I was lost, Jace, you know that. With Callie, I could be saved. Even after all the years between our marriage in now, I thought I could win her over. I won't let you muddy the waters here, Jace. I'll kill you first."

"You can try."

Each man looked as if he was about to go for his revolver but waiting for the other to move first, figuring he was a second faster or a bit more accurate than his foe. People nervously though excitedly began to gather across the street. A few even shouted encouragement for the two to commence fighting.

"Just remember, boy, I knew her first," Van Horn growled. "Even married her."

"And left her. I'd never do that, Travis," the younger man said in tones just as harsh.

Then Callie came running up the street, her skirts swirling in the dust, until she stopped between the two hard-faced men as they were expressing more disdain for the other. Her daughter, Annie, wasn't far behind and hid behind a pole holding up the portico roof of a butcher shop.

"That's enough, you two," Callie snapped, anger coloring her beautiful, usually pale face.

"We were just—" Van Horn said somewhat contritely.

"I know what you were just doing. My friend told me

she heard you two arguin' over me, and I won't have it. It makes me godawful mad."

"Callie, I—" Coppersmith started.

"Hush, Jace." She put on a lighter face than she really felt. "You two know I care about both of you. Making a decision was difficult at best. I thought I had made it but you comin' back, Jace, has put a different light on it. Now I'm not even sure I want to make that choice."

"I was your first, Callie," Van Horn said.

"And you deserted me for three years."

"I didn't desert you, Callie. I—"

"You were gone for three years, Travis. I had no idea where you'd gone. I thought you were dead, and then you suddenly appear again? Not a way to keep a girl's heart." She turned her gaze on Coppersmith. "And you running off on your fiancée. What is it with men always running away on the women they're supposed to be in love with?"

The two men, as tough as any who rode the west, hung their heads like recalcitrant schoolboys caught pulling a girl's pigtails. Coppersmith and Van Horn looked at each other. The latter's hand inched toward one of his Remingtons again.

"You don't want to do that, Travis," Coppersmith warned.

"Afraid I'll beat you?" Van Horn sneered.

"Nope. Afraid *I'll* beat *you*."

"Stop it right now!" Callie snapped, eyes flashing red with anger. "You're acting like children. Did you two fools ever bother to think that I have some say in this matter? Did you?"

Each man shook his head.

"I didn't think so. I ain't some prize to be won like I was a fat turkey at a shootin' match. I bet you never thought that I might want both of you. Or neither of you. I'm a woman, by God, and a mighty good one if I got two men like you fightin' over me. It's true, Travis, that we were married but like Jace said, you went and left me."

"I didn't—"

"Hush. And you, Jace, you're a fine man, much like Travis, strong, good at heart mostly, helpful to folks who ain't used to trouble. But you're young…"

"I ain't that young," Coppersmith mumbled defensively.

Callie looked at him for a moment, then nodded. "I reckon you ain't, but you're some years younger than this old lady."

"You're far from an old lady. Callie. You're—" Coppersmith protested.

"Just hush, Jace. Like Travis, you also left your woman behind."

"I had reason," Coppersmith said, almost pouting.

"Me, too," Van Horn threw in.

"Maybe you men think so, but we women might not. Men don't think about us women. You just do what you want with no thought as to what we might think. No, you just leave us at home, worrying about you and wondering whether you'll ever come home or die in some darn gunfight somewhere, leavin' us and our children alone."

"What you need to do, Callie—" Van Horn started.

"What I need to do is none of your concern. You should be worryin' about what *you* should do. And Jace, too. Which is to leave off buttin' heads with each other until I've made up my mind about what to do about this situation. And if either of you starts to cause trouble, I'll send both of you packin'. Now, Travis, you go on to the

Iron Horse, and Jace, you head to the Stone Pony. Then go on to wherever you're stayin'."

"When will you...?" Coppersmith began.

"When I do. And not a moment before. Now get, both of you."

"But, Callie," Van Horn said.

"Get I said!" She stood with hands on hips, glaring from one tough bounty hunter to the other, both of whom withered somewhat under her gaze.

Coppersmith turned and began to shuffle off, trying to ignore the snorts of derision from some of the men in the crowd.

Suddenly Annie screeched, "Mr. Jace!"

Coppersmith began turning and going down to one knee, reaching for a Colt. He had not made it all the way around when a slug caught him in the right pectoral muscle. Callie screamed. Coppersmith fired as he went down, seeing that he had hit Van Horn just before his own head hit the ground. Callie shrieked again.

Coppersmith tied to roll over so he could push himself up, his back hunched against another shot he figured was coming. He managed to get partway up and was preparing to fire again when he saw Van Horn stagger, then fall as a gunshot rang out.

Screaming his name, Annie came running toward Coppersmith and he knocked her to the ground with an arm and held the squirming girl there as he frantically tried to see where the shot had come from. With the crowd scattering, he spotted a man with a still smoking pistol in hand. Shaking from the shock and loss of blood, Coppersmith took aim and fired. He heard another shot and glanced over to see Van Horn had fired from where he lay on the ground.

But the man who had shot Van Horn was down.

"Stay here, Annie," Coppersmith ordered. He staggered to where the man with the revolver lay and saw that he was near death. "Who the hell are you?" Coppersmith asked as he kicked the man's gun away.

"Billy Biddle," the man said.

"And relation to Bucky?"

"Brother. You two killed my brother."

"The son of a bitch deserved it. So do you, you bastard." He cocked his Colt but realized Biddle was dead.

Coppersmith hurried as fast as he could to where Van Horn lay. A doctor and lawmen led by Ford County Sheriff George Hinkle were already at Van Horn's side.

Annie was tentatively heading toward him. "Get her out of here, Callie!" he roared.

Callie hauled a still screaming daughter away down the street a little ways. But she could not leave, not while the two men she loved were bleeding, even if it meant Annie had to see more of the horror, but at least she would ensure it wasn't too close up.

Despite his weakness, Coppersmith managed to shove his way through the law and kneel at Van Horn's side. "How is he, Doc?"

The physician shook his head but said nothing.

"Why'd you shoot me, Travis? It was you, wasn't it, before that bastard fired?"

"No, I wouldn't do that Jace. Even these days as bad as I've been the last few years."

"Oh, lordy, I shot you then for no reason."

Callie pushed in to kneel on the other side of Van Horn, leaving Annie in the firm grip of a friend. She gasped at Coppersmith's statement.

"It's all right. You didn't know. I would've done the same thing. And I deserved it after bein' such a scoundrel for so long and treatin' you and Reese and everybody else like dogs for so long now. I was comin' around when I come callin' on Callie again, and she started to favor me, but then I began to go back to what I'd been recently when you came along. I'm plumb ashamed of that. Reckon it's far too late to offer any apologies for you, both of you, to accept 'em. But I offer 'em anyway."

"I forgive you, Travis," Callie said, tears flowing freely and plentifully.

"I do, too, Travis. You were a special friend to me. Despite the way you've been the last few years, I never forgot that, and always hoped your head would clear again and be the Travis Van Horn of old."

"Thanks, my old friend. Take care of Callie." He looked at the woman and almost managed a smile. "And you take good care of Jace if you'll have him. He's a damn good man. He's—"

He was gone.

The doctor reached over and slid his hands over Van Horn's eyes, closing them. "Now, let's look at you, Jace is it?"

"But I—"

"No buts. You're bad wounded but you'll live if you get treatment right now."

"Go with him, Jace," Callie said, still crying heavily. "I'll see to arrangements for Travis."

———

UNDER THE INFLUENCE OF ETHER, Coppersmith was unaware of the doctor having removed the bullet, cleaned the wound, applied some Lugol's solution, and bandaged it. And not long after he awoke, Hinkle showed up.

"Need to hear what happened," the lawman said.

Coppersmith explained who Biddle was, what had brought the man to do what he had.

"I heard about the child bein' taken," Hinkle said, "though I wasn't in law enforcement then. It's too bad this fella wasn't paid back before he shot your friend. Any man who takes a child like this man's brother did deserves whatever punishment we can give him. And that goes for any kin that protect him."

The wounded man nodded.

"Well, looks like I'm not needed here any longer," the lawman said. "No laws've been broken and if any fool was to ask, this was clearly a case of self-defense. Get well, Mr. Coppersmith."

A few minutes after Hinkle left, Callie and Annie came into the doctor's office. "Hi, Mr. Jace!" Annie said brightly though she was rather pasty-faced and looked scared.

"Hi, Annie. You know, you have to stop callin' me Mr. Jace. Especially if—" He looked hopefully at Callie.

She smiled. "You should start calling him Pa, Annie."

A LOOK AT: BLOOD TRAIL

THE COMPLETE WESTERN SERIES

Times were tough in the Old West, and Travis VanHorn can attest to that.

Humiliated and left to die by a band of ruthless outlaws, Travis VanHorn is saved by a man even harder than those who nearly killed him. From that moment on, Travis finds himself knee deep in suspenseful adventure.

The body count continues to rise, the stakes get higher and the battles get tougher. But Travis will follow the blood trail until the end – possibly his end.

The Blood Trail Series includes: Blood Trail, Blood Feud and Blood Vengeance.

AVAILABLE NOW

ABOUT THE AUTHOR

John Legg has published more than 55 novels, all on Old West themes. Legg holds a B.A. in Communications and an M.S. in Journalism, and is a copy editor with The New York Times News Service.

Since his first two books, Legg has, under his own name, entertained the Western audience with many more tales of man's fight for independence on the Western frontier. In addition, he has had published several historical novels set in the Old West. Among those are WAR AT BENT'S FORT and BLOOD AT FORT BRIDGER.

In addition, Legg has, under pseudonyms, contributed to the RAMSEYS, a series that was published by Berkley, and was the sole author of the eight books in the SADDLE TRAMP series for HarperPaperbacks. He also was the sole author of WILDGUN, an eight-book adult Western series from Berkley/Jove.

CPSIA information can be obtained
at www.ICGtesting.com
Printed in the USA
BVHW082223140223
658491BV00013B/975